Charles Dickens and the Street Children of London

by ANDREA WARREN

Houghton Mifflin Books for Children
Houghton Mifflin Harcourt
Boston   New York   2011

For my boys, Elijah, Kaden, and Matti

Houghton Mifflin Books for Children is an imprint of Houghton Mifflin Harcourt Publishing Company.

www.hmhbooks.com
Book design by YAY! Design
The text of this book is set in Bodoni Old Face.

Library of Congress Cataloging-in-Publication Control Number 2011003450

ISBN 978-0-547-39574-6

Manufactured in Singapore
TWP 10 9 8 7 6 5 4 3 2 1
4500306811

Photo Credits
Bridgeman Art Library: 12, 15, 25, 30, 36, 65, 88, 116, 117, 118, 143; Getty Images/
Apic: 7, 18; Getty Images/George Cruikshank: 57, 60; Getty Images/English School:
32, 120; Getty Images/Hulton Archive: 6, 9, 21, 44, 59, 68, 78, 90, 137; Getty Images/
Mark Kauffman: 47, 131, 133; Getty Images/Science and Society Picture Library: 5,
16; Getty Images/Time Life Pictures: 39, 76, 97, 107, 110; Getty Images/Various: 10
(Hulton Collection), 23 (Royal Photographic Society), 41 (Fine Art Photographic),
51 (General Photographic Agency), 53 (John Thomson), 72 (Felix Man), 80 (William
Hogarth), 82 (Three Lions), 91 (Rischgitz), 93 (Henry Guttmann), 100 (Popperfoto),
112 (John Leech), 121 (Joseph Mallord William Turner), 127 (William Grundy), 136
(James Bacon), 139 (FPC), 140 (After Franz Xavier Winterhalter), 142 (Jerry Cooke),
142 (Daniel Berehulak); Andrea Warren: 63, 103, 145.

Contents

COMPASSION FOR DEPRIVED CHILDREN
WAS DOMINANT ALWAYS
IN CHARLES DICKENS' THOUGHTS AND SYMPATHIES.

—Ivor Brown, *Dickens in His Time*

Introduction

Perhaps because I grew up in the security of a large family in a small town, I have always been sympathetic to the plight of homeless children. My desire to help led me to adopt a child orphaned by the Vietnam War. As a result, my nonfiction books for young readers have covered the topic of children orphaned by war, and also the estimated 250,000 homeless children who between 1854 and 1930 rode orphan trains across America in search of new families.

While working in London for a few months several years ago, I became interested in how the British had dealt with homeless children in the past. In the nineteenth century, grinding poverty led to tens of thousands of abandoned and orphaned children living on the streets of both London and New York City. Today both the American and British governments have well-established programs to help the poor and unfortunate, but back then it was left largely to charitable organizations, and assistance was often hit or miss.

The orphan train movement helped many children in this

country find homes, but a similar program wasn't an option in England, for most people in the upper classes would not have taken in a child from the streets or slums. The British believed back then that you were rightfully born into a certain class and you belonged there. Many gave grudgingly to charity and felt that the poorest of the poor—usually children—should accept their lot in life.

It was the writer Charles Dickens who changed everything for these children and for the poor in general. His accomplishment was astonishing. In all his writings, he portrayed the poor so sympathetically that the upper classes were moved to begin the slow process of correcting the social ills responsible for much of the suffering of the lower classes.

In Dickens' stories, ragged youngsters are always there on the fringes—begging, scrambling for work, sleeping in parks and under bridges, trying to keep body and soul together. He portrayed these children so touchingly because he had nearly become one of them. Though he was born into the middle class, through a series of family crises Dickens learned what it was like to be a hungry, powerless child who had to labor long hours for low wages. He learned that most of the poor were good, deserving people who were held down and exploited by the upper classes. He never forgot it.

Through his own hard work and in spite of little formal education, Dickens became a masterful writer. People of every class embraced his stories. The poor claimed him as their spokesman and hero. The upper classes loved him just as much. Few realized that he was subtly influencing them to take up the causes he promoted in his plots, whether it was improving the workhouses, educating slum children, bettering conditions for workers, or cleaning up the slums.

All in all, Charles Dickens was a more powerful catalyst for change than any queen, prime minister, or politician. He is known as one of history's greatest reformers.

As you read about Dickens and what he and others accomplished for London's poorest children, I hope you will be inspired to use your own talents, whatever they are, to ease the suffering of the less fortunate all over this planet. Like Charles Dickens, you too can help make the world a better place.

Chapter 1

The Man in the Shadows

IN THE YEAR 1835, London was full of energy. Every day the city's dirt and cobblestone streets filled with traffic early in the morning. Stray dogs nipped at the heels of the horses or donkeys pulling carts, carriages, and coaches that vied for space with the sheep and pigs being herded to market. People were everywhere. They roamed the street markets in search of bargains. Some visited shops or stopped into

Well known to Dickens was London's giant Smithfield Market, shown here in 1855. Dickens was critical of the market's location in the heart of the city because of its filth and noise.

saloons to enjoy a pint of ale or glass of gin. Sidewalk gamblers lured customers into card games. Musicians, acrobats, jugglers, and actors performed, hoping for tips from passersby. Peddlers called out their offerings of fried oysters, fresh flowers, old clothes, newspapers, or meat pies. The aromas of hot coffee, grilled meat, and fried bread mixed with the odors of people, horses, tobacco, and coal tar.

Only when it began to get dark did the noise die down. The peddlers left. Tailors, butchers, and other shopkeepers locked their doors and headed for home. Soon, only taverns and eating houses were still open, adding a faint glow to the dim light provided by streetlamps. Many streets had no light, and the dozens of lanes and alleyways that threaded off them were pitch black.

It was down these lanes and alleys that the poor lived, crowded into dingy, dirty tenements. The poorest of the poor—those who had so far managed to stay out of the despicable workhouses that were their last resort—lived on the streets. Most sought out dark spots, feeling safest when they could not be seen.

A slender young man, stylishly dressed and wearing a proper coat and hat, often walked the city at night. He knew the poor were there in the shadows. Once he had been a child with nothing. His world had fallen apart when his father was arrested for debt and put in prison. He had been separated

Shown here at age twenty-seven, Dickens was a careful observer of people. He had a special interest in children and put them in all of his stories.

from his family and forced to work long hours in a damp, dismal warehouse to support himself. Sometimes he had been cold and hungry and so full of misery that he could not picture his own future.

But now he walked because he enjoyed it. He moved at a brisk pace for hours at a time, thinking through problems bothering him with his work, but also paying careful attention to what was going on around him and to the people he saw. Occasionally he stopped to write in a notebook. During his late-evening walks in the poorer districts of the city, he regularly came across homeless people who were dressed in rags and

huddled together for warmth. Seeing children in this condition was especially upsetting, and fueled his anger at society's indifference toward them. He vowed to use his own knowledge of wretched poverty to shame the powerful into action.

Back at his writing desk, his pen on fire, he worked on the sketches and stories that would force others to see what he saw, and feel what he had felt. People were noticing. They watched for his name, and when they saw the byline *Charles Dickens,* they started to read.

Though seemingly invisible to the upper classes, poor children were everywhere in London. Dickens was acutely aware of them and highly sensitive to their suffering.

Chapter 2

The Poor People of London

WHEN TWENTY-THREE-YEAR-OLD Charles Dickens was beginning to make his name as a journalist and author in 1835, London was a city of glittering wealth and dismal poverty, of light and shadow, of daytime delights and dreadful night.

Dickens saw these startling contrasts every day. The British Empire ruled half the world. London was its capital, and with more than a million people, it was Europe's largest city. A center of business and industry, it was home to museums, concert halls, and parks. Wealthy people lived in elegant mansions, attended by a bevy of servants. The royal family had several fine palaces, each with stately gardens.

Yet much of the city was just as it had been centuries earlier: primitive, overcrowded, filthy, and violent. The average life span of a Londoner was only twenty-seven years. For the poor, it was twenty-two—and these could be brutal years, played out against a landscape of despair.

As Dickens was all too aware, London had a staggering

Gin was considered the national drink in Dickens' day. In this gin palace, even young children drank alcohol.

number of poor people. They eked out a living however they could, but many simply had no way to support themselves. Dickens had heard the stories of old people who took poison to end their miserable lives, and he knew that every morning the police found dead babies in trash cans, cast aside by hapless parents who could not feed them.

On his daily walks, Dickens passed taverns and gin palaces where poor people drank themselves into early graves. Many of the poor were victims of violence. Some died of starvation. Disease was rampant in the city, and the poor succumbed in great numbers from typhoid fever, diarrhea, and smallpox. Smoke from the city's hundreds of thousands of coal-burning chimneys melded into a grimy fog that hung in the air, and coal dust caused lung problems for even the very young.

In spite of the awful conditions, the poor kept coming to the city, seeking work in the massive factories and mills. They toiled in the shipyards, on the docks, and in the outdoor markets. So many sought each available position that employers could demand they labor as many as sixteen hours a day, six or even seven days a week. Wages were so low that poor workers could barely support themselves, much less a family. Dickens knew that work conditions could be dangerous

Shipbuilding was a huge industry in Dickens' London,
where half the world's ships were built. For workers, the hours were long,
the pay low, and the jobs hard and often dangerous.

and that injured workers received no assistance. The families of workers killed on the job were given nothing.

Housing in the overcrowded city was in critically short supply. The poor were jammed into huge tenements, sometimes a dozen people living in a single small room. If the room even had a bed, several people at a time took turns sleeping in it while others slept on the floor. The lucky ones might have a small coal-burning stove to keep them warm and to cook whatever food they had scrounged. Candles, or perhaps an oil lamp, provided the only other source of light.

Unlike the gentrified neighborhood where Dickens lived, there was little or no clean drinking water in the slums. Usually there was a pump somewhere in the area, but pump water came from the Thames (pronounced "Tems") River and was brownish and foul tasting, for the city's sewage was dumped into the river. As a result, both adults and children drank beer and gin. Filthy outdoor privies for going to the bathroom were shared by everyone in the slums. They contributed to the overpowering stench that permeated the tenement district— a combination of sewage, animal droppings, and the vast sea of people who had no way to wash themselves or their belongings. Lice and fleas infested hair, clothing, and straw mattresses. Rats and roaches competed with dogs and children for crumbs of food.

Hardest for Dickens to witness was the suffering of children. When he walked through the slums, he saw them everywhere. The poor rarely had access to reliable birth control, so families could be large, even though at least half the children died before their fifth birthday. Those who survived were usually sickly but still had to work. Education was for the upper classes; poor children had to earn their keep.

By age ten, both boys and girls labored long hours in mills and factories alongside adults. At home, their youngest siblings followed the coal carts, picking up bits that dropped on the ground to feed the fire. Girls of six or seven cared for younger brothers and sisters. Mothers who were hired out as washerwomen took daughters along to help with the back-breaking work. Some women also did sewing and taught their young daughters to thread needles and tie knots. By

In spite of the sentimentality of this illustration, these little flower sellers could be severely punished if they did not successfully sell all of their flowers or if they ruined some.

three in the morning, adults who worked as peddlers roused children out of sleep to walk several miles to a marketplace where cartloads of freshly picked vegetables were arriving from the countryside. Regardless of the weather, boys and girls helped sort through lettuce, cabbages, onions, turnips, herbs, or other produce. Little hands learned to pull off rotten leaves, stuffing them in their pockets to take home to make soup.

By the time they were eight, some girls spent their days walking busy streets, trying to sell apples or grapes, shoelaces, matches, flowers, or eggs. They might have younger brothers or sisters in tow. No one looked twice at a young girl holding a baby in one arm, carrying a basket on the other, with one or more small children following behind. Her voice would grow hoarse from trying to be heard above the din of the streets as she approached people, begging them to buy from her.

The hours dragged by. The baby cried, the other children did too, longing for food and naps, and in winter, for warmth. They were splashed by wagons. The girl worried about older boys stealing from her. She feared that the little ones would get stepped on by a horse or get lost in the crowds.

It must have amazed a child like this when she saw wealthy people go by in carriages pulled by teams of matching horses. How could such a life exist? To be carried along by horses, above the muddy streets, attended by footmen, and dressed in fine clean clothes! The poor were not allowed to hawk their wares on exclusive streets, but they might catch glimpses of grand homes when gates opened to admit carriages. Servants helped their masters and mistresses step down, holding umbrellas above them if it was raining. Other opened doors for them. It was a world the poor could only dream of. They understood that people were born into a certain station in life. Good or bad, you deserved it. Unless you could elevate yourself by becoming rich, you were expected to accept it.

When at last the girl had sold her goods or it grew too dark to work, she went back to the small, crowded room that was home. Many adults worked until ten at night, and there might be little or no food waiting. And though she was inside and away from the dangers of the street, other dangers might await. Many adults were alcoholics. Nobody intervened when men beat their wives or children. Little ones faced the prospect of beatings and abuse if they had not sold enough during the day, or if they had slipped in an icy puddle and ruined their wares—or for no reason except that they could not defend themselves.

Life was as difficult for boys as it was for girls. Until they were big and strong enough to compete for men's jobs, they worked as peddlers, just as the girls did, or ran errands or cleaned stables. Hoping for tips, they worked as crossing sweeps, using a small broom to brush mud, slush, animal droppings, or garbage out of the way of people who were getting out of carriages.

London's hundreds of thousands of chimneys had to be

cleaned regularly to work efficiently. While lots of jobs were dangerous, this was one of the most hazardous. Many chimneys were so narrow and had such tight bends and turns that only small boys could get through them. Master chimney sweeps recruited homeless boys from the streets, or "purchased" them from orphanages that were glad to be rid of them.

A boy climbed up by grabbing braces placed in the bricks, using a brush or his clothes to dislodge clumps of coal dust. He was quickly coated with soot that made him cough. To goad him to work faster, his master might start a little fire in the chimney grate, sending heat and smoke upward, forcing the boy to hurry to the top. An alarming number of boys died in the chimneys. Sometimes they got stuck and suffocated before they could be rescued. Others lost their footing and fell to their death.

Both boys and girls scavenged along the Thames River. Dickens saw them when he walked there. Twice daily at low tide, regardless of the weather, they waded into the filthy water to search for a nail, a button, an old shoe, a tin can—anything

Chimney sweeps faced many hazards, including falling, getting stuck, or suffocating. Climbing upward, the sweep loosened built-up soot, knocking it into a bag. When he finally emerged from the chimney, his clothes, skin, and lungs were coated with coal dust.

sellable that had dropped from ships and barges and washed ashore. They also begged, picked pockets, and stole food. When the outdoor markets closed for the day, street children grabbed any bits of food left behind. Some boys turned to hard crime—robbery and murder. Girls as young as twelve might be lured into prostitution. And still they were dogged by grinding, never-ending poverty.

Dickens was outraged that the government offered no assistance, instead decreeing that the poor were the responsibility of church parishes. Every poor person knew to which church parish he or she belonged and what charity that parish offered. Parishes also operated workhouses to care for the poor

The poor line up for a bowl of soup and piece of bread at a charitable soup kitchen in London in 1867.

who had nowhere else to go. But life was so hard in the work-house that some chose to take their chances on the streets.

This included children. They joined swarms of other children who were orphans or had been turned out by uncaring parents or had run away because of abuse. They slept in door-ways and stables and on park benches. Dressed in rags, often without shoes, they huddled together for warmth, sleeping in snatches, wary, worried, never comfortable, their frail limbs stiff and their lips turning blue when the night air grew cold. They ate garbage and stole from other children or from the elderly. They pleaded with every passerby for a handout. If they were lucky enough to encounter someone as sympathetic as Charles Dickens, they would get a coin. But such luck was rare.

London had tens of thousands of street children at the time Charles Dickens was starting to write the essays, short stories, and novels that would help change British attitudes toward the poor. He always included children in his stories, and a few of the most memorable were boys trying to find their way in life, often victimized by adults or by a society that viewed them with disdain because of their lowly station.

It would be many years before the world learned the story of Dickens' own boyhood, and before even his wife and children realized that these boys in his books seemed so real because they were different parts of Dickens himself. Moreover, many of the hardships they suffered were based on Dickens' own experiences growing up.

Chapter 3

The Early Years

FOR THE FIRST TEN years of his life, the future novelist knew nothing about poor children in London. Charles John Huffman Dickens was born in 1812 in Portsmouth, England, the second child and first son of John and Elizabeth Dickens. He had his mother's brown hair and large, expressive hazel-colored eyes, and he was an inquisitive child with an excellent memory for fact and detail. Once he learned how, he was often observed reading, even when other children were playing outside.

Dickens once said he'd had nothing ever left to him but relatives. Indeed, he ended up supporting his mother, Elizabeth Dickens, shown here, from the time he was a young man until her death at age seventy-four.

Both of his parents were gifted storytellers and passed this ability to their son. Like his mother, Dickens was a talented mimic. He acted out scenes from stories, playing all the parts, using a distinctive voice for each. He also wrote plays and recruited neighborhood children to act in them. He loved to hear people applaud for him. His older sister, Fanny, was musically gifted, and sometimes the two of them sang songs together. One time they even performed in a local tavern, and everyone cheered when they finished.

The family lived in small country towns, where the pace of life was slow and pleasant. When Dickens was five they settled in the village of Chatham. It was close to the market town of Rochester, on the Medway River, and had an old castle dating back to the Norman Conquest, and an ancient cathedral. Young Dickens gazed in fascination at the hospital ships and prison ships anchored out in the Medway, and he heard spine-tingling stories of escaped convicts. Because Rochester was a navy town, he saw soldiers and sailors on the streets. Sometimes traveling fairs came through and his father took him to see actors perform dramas and comedies. These places, these people, and these events fed his imagination.

His father, who worked as a clerk in the navy pay office, was a man of great charm and excellent manners. John Dickens loved to entertain, and at Christmas the Dickens home was filled with feasting, music, dancing, games, and storytelling. He was devoted to his wife and children, and they to him. Charles

Dickens said that when he was sick as a child, he always knew his father would be right by his side, where "he watched night and day, unweariedly and patiently."

But even his beloved father could not erase the sorrow the whole family felt when two children, born after Dickens, died while very young. Nor could Dickens' father ease the searing pain the boy occasionally suffered in his side, especially at times of great stress. Indeed, it was the father who often created this stress. John Dickens' parents were servants and he had grown up in the servants' quarters of a large estate, observing the wealthy master's lifestyle. On his salary as a clerk for the navy, John Dickens could support his family in moderate comfort, but he aspired to the finer things in life. He dressed as a gentleman—though he was not of that class—and he purchased whatever indulgences he fancied. Because of this, the family was always in debt.

Like his father, the boy Dickens aspired to living well, but unlike his father, he understood that you had to earn what you wanted to buy. There was a house near Rochester that Dickens admired and would go out of his way to see. Gads Hill Place was grander than any other home in the area. "I thought it was the most beautiful house," Dickens recalled. "My father, seeing me so extraordinarily fond of it, often said to me, 'If you are persevering, and work hard, you might some day come to live in it.'"

Could a boy like him, a lower-middle-class boy in a family

where money was always a problem, ever live in such a fine house? Young as he was, Dickens knew two things for certain: first, he wanted an education; second, he wanted to make enough money that he was never in debt—enough money that he could one day own Gads Hill Place.

Gads Hill Place, the grand home Dickens dreamed as a boy of one day owning, is now a school. Because of its strong connection to the author, visitors may take tours.

In 1822 when Dickens was ten, the family moved to the outskirts of London. Dickens' father still worked for the navy pay office and hoped the city would offer more opportunity. The family now had five children and also employed an orphan girl from the Chatham workhouse to help with the heavy housework. Because London was so crowded and housing so expensive, they could only afford a small house on a shabby street. A distant relation squeezed in with them, taking up precious space in the crowded little house, but contributing badly needed rent.

Before the move, the Dickens family had lived comfortably. But, wrote Dickens, "within a single year all this was changed. . . . Now, it was all coarse and common." He added, "It is the most miserable thing to feel ashamed of home."

Though already in debt, John Dickens borrowed money so Fanny could attend the Royal Academy of Music to study piano. Dickens missed his sister, who lived at the academy. But while his sister got an excellent education, Dickens got none. School cost money, and Dickens' parents could not afford tuition for him. Dickens knew that he could not get ahead in life without an education, but his pleas to his parents got him nowhere. He said that his father "appeared to have utterly lost at this time the idea of educating me at all and to have utterly put from him the notion that I had any claim upon him in that regard, whatever."

Dickens escaped into a world of fantasy. He built a toy theater and acted out plays. His father had a small library of classic books—Chaucer, Shakespeare, Defoe, Fielding, Swift, Cervantes, and others—and Dickens read them all. He wrote short sketches about people in his neighborhood and took long walks through the busy city. London was both dangerous and fascinating. Dickens encountered the rich and poor engaged in the drama of life. He was accosted by aggressive peddlers wanting to sell him something. He stopped to watch street musicians and jugglers. He had to beware of pickpockets and thieves. And wherever he walked, he saw street children.

At home, he tried to help by "making myself useful in the work of the little house; and looking after my younger brothers and sister . . . and going on such poor errands as arose out of our poor way of living." His mother tried to open a day school, and one of Dickens' tasks was to distribute flyers advertising it. But no students came and the family slid still further into debt. Because they owed everybody money, Dickens recalled, "We got on very badly with the butcher and baker [and] very often we had not too much for dinner."

The relative living with them moved out when he became the manager of a small warehouse factory.

When Dickens moved to London at age ten, he saw his first street children. This homeless child is trying to sleep outside.

He suggested that Dickens, who had just turned twelve, come to work there. Dickens' parents did not ask their son if he wanted to—they merely informed him that he would. Dickens was shocked. All he wanted was to be allowed to go to school, but his parents had other plans. "My father and mother were quite satisfied," he recalled. "They could hardly have been more so if I had been twenty years of age, distinguished at a grammar school, and going to Cambridge."

Chapter 4

A Working-Class Boy

ON HIS FIRST DAY OF WORK at Warren's Blacking Factory, Charles Dickens was horrified to learn that he would be doing common labor alongside working-class boys. He had been raised to believe that the lower classes were undeserving of anything better, and were so dirty that he could be contaminated by them. The realization that he was now one of them was almost more humiliation than he could stand. "No words can express the secret agony of my soul as I sunk into this companionship," he said.

Dickens' childhood abruptly ended when he became a bootblack boy at a factory similar to these warehouses along the Thames River. His association with Bob Fagin and other working-class boys helped change his views of the poor.

The blacking factory was located in a rundown warehouse that was directly on the banks of the Thames River, allowing waste matter to be dumped straight into the water. Dickens described it as a "crazy, tumble-down old house." It had rotted floors, and he would never forget "the old grey rats swarming down in the cellars, and the sound of their squeaking and scuffling coming up the stairs at all times, and the dirt and decay of the place." Because it was by the river, it was freezing and damp in the winter, and hot and humid in the summer.

The factory made bootblack polish that people used to clean and shine shoes and boots. Dickens' job was to sit at a little table and tie string around small jars filled with blacking, then paste a label on each one—tedious, repetitive tasks that he performed for ten hours a day, six days a week.

As upset as he was by all of this, things were worse at home. A few days after he became a bootblack boy, his father was arrested for unpaid debt and sent to debtors' prison, where he would have to stay until his debts were somehow paid—even though he couldn't work while he was in prison. John Dickens mournfully proclaimed that the sun had set upon him forever. "I really thought his heart was broken and mine too," Dickens said.

The Marshalsea Prison was gloomy, crowded, and noisy. Each prisoner's room had a bed, a fireplace, and a small window so high on the wall that it was impossible to see anything but the sky. On Dickens' first visit, he reported, he and his father both "cried very much. And he told me, I remember, to take warning by the Marshalsea, and to observe that if a man had twenty pounds a year, and spent nineteen pounds nineteen shillings and sixpence, he would be happy; but that a shilling spent the other way would make him wretched." Years later, when Dickens wrote his great novel *David Copperfield,* he placed one of his characters in debtors' prison and had him repeat these very words to young David Copperfield.

Dickens' small earnings were of some help to his mother, but in a very short while she could no longer pay the rent. To get money she began selling family belongings. Dickens recalled, "Almost everything, by degrees, was sold or pawned. My father's books went first. I carried them, one after another, to a bookstall . . . and sold them for whatever they would bring." One day a wagon arrived to cart away the furniture. The family camped out in the bare parlor. The workhouse girl found another job.

When there was nothing more to sell or pawn, Elizabeth Dickens faced the choice of either moving her family to a workhouse or into the Marshalsea to share John Dickens' eight-by-twelve-foot prison cell. Dreading the hardships of the workhouse, she chose the prison, taking the three youngest children with her. Fanny remained at the Royal Academy of Music, fearful that she would be asked to leave at any moment since her father could no longer borrow money to pay her tuition.

Dickens became a lodger in the cramped home of an elderly lady who boarded children. There he shared a small room with two other boys, paying for his space from his meager earnings, giving his mother what money he could and using the rest to buy food. He awoke early each morning and arrived at the prison just as the gates were unlocked. He saw his family, then headed to work, often returning in the evening to see them again. On Sundays he met Fanny at her school and together they went to the Marshalsea to spend the day, leaving before the prison bell rang its warning at ten p.m.

Sometimes at the Marshalsea, Dickens watched his younger siblings playing in the prison yard—a scene he would later put in one of his books. Several of his fictional characters would spend time in the Marshalsea. One, a girl named Little Dorrit, would live there with her father. The idea of prisons, of circumstances of life making one feel imprisoned, or of houses seeming like prisons, would permeate Dickens' writings forever after.

Lying awake at night, he must have wondered how so much bad could have happened to his family. He was lonely and forlorn. He was twelve years old and on his own, receiving, he said, "no advice, no counsel, no encouragement, no consolation, no support, from anyone that I can call to mind."

He could never ever have imagined that one day he would be the most famous writer in the world, that he would own the beautiful Gads Hill house near Rochester, and that several of the streets he now walked to get to the prison would be named for fictional characters that he would bring to life in books.

Neither could this boy, who was not allowed to go to school, have believed that one day, on the very spot where his grim boarding house now stood, there would be a school where children received the education he so wanted—and that it would be called the Charles Dickens Primary School.

Each day, Dickens walked three miles through London's grimy streets to get to work. He smelled coal tar, tobacco, and the foods sold in street stalls—hot chestnuts, oysters, baked potatoes, fish, meat pies, and hot coffee. Because of London's huge docks and shipyards, he saw travelers from all over the world and heard every possible language. He stopped to peer into shop windows at stationery, books, newspapers, buttons, pens, ribbons and lace, gloves, hats, and boots. He was distracted by dogfights, and the ringing of the huge bell of Saint Paul's Cathedral. He stepped around drunken men, women, and even children staggering out of the city's numerous gin palaces. He passed Newgate Prison and gazed in fascinated horror at the bodies on display of criminals who had been recently hanged. Sometimes he sat in the recesses of London Bridge, content to simply watch people go by. Everyone was on the streets, and this imaginative boy was taking mental notes that would one day enrich the stories he would write.

At the factory, Dickens knew that the other workers

wondered about him. "I never said . . . how it was that I came to be there, or gave the least indication of being sorry that I was there. That I suffered in secret, and that I suffered exquisitely, no one ever knew but I. How much I suffered, it is, as I have said already, utterly beyond my power to tell." Dickens kept to himself. "I did my work. I knew from the first that if I could not do my work as well as any of the rest, I could not hold myself above slight and contempt. I soon became . . . as skillful with my hands as either of the other boys."

Dickens' coworkers didn't know what to make of him: a young gentleman, well spoken and clean, doing the same work they did.

Because he spoke in a more refined manner than his coworkers and tried to stay clean when everyone else was as filthy as the factory, the others referred to him as "the young gentleman."

When one of them sneered at him, Dickens wrote, "Bob Fagin settled him speedily."

Bob Fagin was a rough working-class orphan. He was older and bigger than Dickens, and for some reason felt protective of him. One day Dickens' old problem—that intense pain in his side—flared up. Fagin tried to help. Dickens recalled, "Bob Fagin was very good to me on the occasion of a bad attack of my old disorder. I suffered such excruciating pain that time, that they made a temporary bed of straw . . . and I rolled about on the floor, and Bob filled empty blacking-bottles with hot water, and applied relays of them to my side half the day."

By quitting time, Dickens felt better. "But Bob . . . did not like the idea of my going home alone, and took me under his protection. I was too proud to let him know about the prison; and after making several efforts to get rid of him, to all of which Bob Fagin in his goodness was deaf, we shook hands on the steps of a house near Southwark Bridge . . . making believe that I lived there . . . in case of his looking back, I knocked at the door . . . and asked, when the woman opened it, if that was Mr. Robert Fagin's house."

Dickens never forgot the kindness shown him by Fagin and his other coworkers. As he got to know them, he realized that in spite of what he'd been taught, they were real people with real feelings—just like him.

Every day Dickens used his earnings to purchase bread and cheese, the cheap foods of the lower classes. If he had any extra money, he sometimes stopped at a vendor's stall to buy a sweet raisin cake he liked very much. A few times he went into a pub and had a glass of beer. On one occasion he treated himself to a full meal at a chophouse and even left the waiter a tip. Food was always on his mind, and his stomach often rumbled with hunger. His short afternoon breaks were no exception: "When I had money enough I used to go to a

Poor children like these, living in the narrow lanes and alleys of London's slums, reminded Dickens that he might well become one of them. (Note the water pump—this lane's only source of water.)

coffee-shop, and have half-a-pint of coffee and a slice of bread and butter. When I had no money I took a turn in Covent Garden Market and stared at the pineapples."

Walking about the city, when he detoured down narrow, twisty streets where the poor lived, he came face-to-face with London's underworld. The filth and odors of the slums were overwhelming. Wherever he turned, he saw painfully thin children dressed in rags, with hopeless eyes. Though despairing of his own situation, he was moved by what he saw and wondered why no one helped the children.

He also realized that if his situation worsened, he could become one of them. He later recalled, "I know I do not exaggerate, unconsciously and unintentionally, the scantiness of my resources and the difficulties of my life. I know that if a shilling or so were given to me by anyone I spent it [on] a dinner or tea. I know that I worked from morning to night, with common men and boys. . . . I know that, but for the mercy of God, I might easily have been, for any care that was taken of me, a little robber or a little vagabond."

Instead, his grandmother died, leaving his father enough money to settle his debts and gain his release from the Marshalsea.

Chapter 5

THE DICKENS FAMILY WAS SOON reunited and living in a new house. Charles Dickens eagerly anticipated leaving the blacking factory behind, returning to school, and getting on with his plans to make something of himself.

But to his dismay, his parents told him they still needed his income and insisted he continue to work—even though his sister Fanny was able to stay at the Royal Academy of Music. When she won several prizes, Dickens was proud of her, but also envious. "I could not bear to think of myself—beyond the reach of all such honorable emulation and success. The tears ran down my face. I felt as if my heart were rent. I prayed, when I went to bed that night, to be lifted out of the humiliation and neglect in which I was."

Shortly after this, Fanny returned home. The academy would no longer accept her father's promise of payment for her tuition. To help the family, she went to work as a music teacher.

The blacking factory was moved to better facilities away from the river. Dickens and Fagin now sat by a front window on the street where the light was good, tying string and pasting labels on the blacking bottles. "Bob Fagin and I had attained great dexterity in tying up the pots. . . . We were so brisk at it, that the people used to stop and look in. Sometimes there would be quite a little crowd there."

One day Dickens saw his father come in the door, where he stood watching his son, the working-class laborer. "I wondered how he could bear it," Dickens recalled.

Indeed, his father could not. John Dickens argued with the factory manager, who sent the boy home. Dickens could not get out of there fast enough. "My father said I should go back no more, and should go to school," Dickens recalled. But his mother, still worried about money, immediately patched up the disagreement with the factory manager and told her son to return. Dickens could not believe what he was hearing. "I do not write resentfully or angrily, for I know how all these things have worked together to make me what I am; but I never afterwards forgot, I never can forget, that my mother was warm for my being sent back."

To Dickens' great relief, his father prevailed.

His first day back in school, Dickens worried what the other boys would think of him. "It seemed to me so long since I had been among such boys, or among any companions of my own age. . . . I was so conscious of having passed through scenes of which they could have no knowledge, and of having acquired experiences foreign to my age, appearance, and conditions as one of them, that I half believed it was an imposture to come there as an ordinary schoolboy. I had become . . . so unused to the sports and games of boys, that I knew I was awkward and inexperienced in the commonest things belonging to them. My mind ran upon what they would think if they knew of my familiar acquaintance with the Marshalsea. What would they say, who made so light on money, if they could know how I

When Dickens finally had the opportunity to return to school, he was a model student and excelled at his studies. But his education was minimal, ending when he was fifteen, and he was largely self-educated.

had scraped my halfpence together, for the purchase of my daily [food]?"

He put his sharp mind to work to make up for several years' lost time. He excelled in his studies, won academic prizes, and wrote stories for the school's literary newspaper. To get the education he craved, he had to tolerate the routine strictness and cruelty of the teachers and the profound ignorance of the headmaster who ran his school. Years later Dickens would attack the British educational system that allowed both mediocrity of instruction and mistreatment of students.

For two years he worked as hard as he could at his studies. Then, just as before, it all ended. In 1827, when Dickens was fifteen, he had to drop out of school and return to work: his father was again seriously in debt. Though England was home to several of the world's greatest universities, there would be no formal education for Charles Dickens. Indeed, John Dickens later commented that his son might be said to have educated himself.

Fortunately Dickens did not have to return to factory work, for a relative recognized his potential and helped him get a job in a law office.

In his position as a junior clerk, he ran errands and copied documents. His mother hoped he would work his way up and perhaps even study to become a lawyer. But Dickens had no patience with the law and all its drudgery. He saw that it created much misery in people's lives, for court cases and appeals could drag on for years. Still, he learned all he could, soaking up detail and closely observing the people around him. Several of them would appear in his novels. So would composites of stuffy lawyers and judges, eccentric clients, and colorful criminals. The law was often biased against the middle and lower classes, and when he became a writer, Dickens landed a blow on behalf of its victims by ridiculing the legal system and the courts with biting, sometimes vicious wit.

Dickens had grown into a handsome teen, slender and of medium height. He wore his brown hair fashionably long and, like his father, always dressed in the latest style. It was his hazel-colored eyes that most impressed others, for they were large, bright, and inquisitive. People also remembered his intense energy, his polite manners, and his cultured way of speaking. He laughed easily and entertained listeners with funny stories in which he took on all the speaking roles, accurately imitating anyone of any class. He was punctual and expected others to be as well. He always paid his debts in full. He was ambitious, determined, compassionate toward those in need, and quick to anger at injustice—qualities that would have a strong impact on his later work as a journalist and author.

Though he kept his childhood difficulties to himself, he never forgot them. And while he loved his parents, he also blamed them. In recalling his boyhood, he was uncertain exactly how long he worked at the blacking factory. His parents never spoke of it, and it was as though it had never happened. Many years later Dickens finally wrote about this traumatizing experience, but only briefly. Yet this was the pivotal event that set him on the course to becoming one of history's great reformers.

Because he associated dirt and ragged garments with the blacking factory, his clothing was always of excellent quality and always clean. Because he had lived with chaos and poverty, his later homes were carefully organized and were places of refuge and calm, where food was plentiful.

People meeting Dickens as a young man never suspected that he had once been a working-class factory boy, for he dressed fashionably and spoke in a cultured manner.

If he found himself walking the streets he once took to the factory, he would start to cry. "I never had the courage to go back to the place where my servitude began," he said. "I never saw it. I could not endure to go near it." If he caught a whiff of the cement glue used on the blacking bottle corks, he was flooded with memories.

Though he told his wife and children nothing of his

childhood trauma, he sometimes dropped hints to others. One appeared in a letter to a friend, the American author Washington Irving, in which he wrote that as a child he had been "a very small and not over-particularly-taken-care-of boy." But he said no more.

He also filled his novels with clues, including references to blacking brushes, blacking bottles, and bootblack advertisements. Several of his characters would share his desperation to rise to a higher class. Pip, the hero of *Great Expectations,* would say, "I knew I was common, and that I wished I was not common." Because he had been hungry, so were some of his characters. Because of all he had experienced, children suffered in his books, just as they did in real life. Because of everything he had seen, some were orphans, some were mistreated, and some died.

He never truly got over the fears, hunger, and anguish he had experienced as a boy. Even when he had a very comfortable income, he worried constantly about money. In his dreams he would forget that he was one of the most famous people in the world and would "wander desolately back to that time in my life."

Chapter 6

Becoming a Writer

On his daily walks through the city, depicted here in 1855, Dickens absorbed street life, learning how people of all classes thought, spoke, and acted.

WHEN CHARLES DICKENS WASN'T working at the law office, he took long daily walks through the busy streets of London, a habit he would continue all his life. He often walked twenty miles or more, learning the city very well—knowledge he would utilize when he became a writer.

He had loved the theater since he was a small boy, and in London, theater was all around him. Most of Dickens' earnings went to his family, but theater tickets were cheap. With the pocket money he kept for himself, he attended plays several times a week, enjoying everything from low farce to classical drama. For a time he thought he might become a professional actor. He decided to try out for a play, but was sick on the day of tryouts and could not go. Had he gotten a part, his life might have taken a different direction.

He left the law office after two years. He had taught himself shorthand and became a freelance court reporter, speedily recording and transcribing everything that happened in court. Next he went to work for a newspaper, covering the British House of Commons. He attended all sessions, recording in shorthand everything that was said and then transcribing it into longhand to be printed in the paper. Recording endless political debates and wrangling soured Dickens on politics, just as he'd already been soured on the law. He would later refer to lawyers and politicians as "a mob of brainless windbags."

At the age of twenty-one, Dickens left behind court reporting to become a political reporter. His job required that he travel through England to cover political meetings. Travel in the 1830s was an ordeal. Though trains went some places, he mostly rode in uncomfortable horse-drawn coaches on bad roads. He visited villages, towns, and cities throughout the country and learned a great deal about English society and people's lives. Because of his own experience, he paid careful attention to the lives of the laboring poor, noting how the British class system kept them in poverty.

Dickens was also the newspaper's theater critic, giving him the excuse to attend as many plays as possible. His very hectic schedule would have exhausted most reporters, but Dickens loved writing about politics and plays. He thrived on all the travel, the tight deadlines, the people he met, and everything he learned. Looking back he would say, "It is to the wholesome training of newspaper work when I was a very young man that I constantly refer my first success."

But while Dickens was forging a reputation as a reporter, his father was still spending more money than he made and the family had to move frequently to avoid creditors. Once again he was arrested for debt. To save his father from returning to prison, Dickens borrowed money, then paid it back as quickly as he could. It's no surprise that money and debt became ongoing themes in his writing.

When Dickens earned a raise at the newspaper, he used this additional income to move into his own lodgings. In his spare time he worked on fictional stories and essays of his own. He was still twenty-one when he got up the nerve to submit a short story to a periodical called the *Monthly Magazine*—but he wasn't brave enough to sign his name. "I had taken, with

Not yet confident enough to use his own name, Dickens anonymously submitted his first story to a weekly magazine, signing it "Boz."

fear and trembling, to authorship," he said. "I wrote a little story in secret . . . which I dropped stealthily one evening at twilight into a dark letter box, in a dark office, up a dark court in Fleet Street."

Dickens never forgot the incredible moment when he opened the next edition of the *Monthly Magazine* and saw his story in print: "I walked down to Westminster Hall, and turned into it for half an hour, because my eyes were so dimmed with joy and pride that they could not bear the street, and were not fit to be seen there."

Soon his stories were appearing in both the *Monthly Magazine* and another periodical. Still not ready to reveal his own name, he signed his stories with the name Boz—a nickname he had given one of his younger brothers. Though he was not paid for his stories, he was learning his craft, finding and training his voice as a writer, and building a

loyal base of readers who soon realized that "Boz" was actually a young man named Charles Dickens.

As he would all his career, he filled his stories with everyday life, observing people at their daily tasks and recording snatches of conversation. He wrote about the markets and courts, festivals and festivities. He often voiced his concern for the poor, writing about crime and the underbelly of the city, about prisons and public hangings, about old people with broken spirits, about the tenements, where windows were stuffed with rags or paper to keep out the cold, and about ragged children pleading for a penny.

Like the great classical authors he admired, he employed drama, comedy, romance, melodrama, and a sense of pathos. In one sketch, titled "The Streets of London at Night," he took readers along on one of his late-evening walks. He wrote of a "wretched woman" who had an infant in her arms. She was singing a cheerful song, hoping that passersby leaving the taverns would give her a penny or two. "A brutal laugh at her weak voice is all she has gained," Dickens wrote. "The tears fall thick and fast down her own pale face; the child is cold and hungry, and its low half-stifled wailing adds to the misery of its wretched mother, as she moans aloud, and sinks despairingly down, on a cold damp doorstep." Dickens speculated that she and the baby could "die of cold and hunger."

He loved names, the odder the better, and kept long lists of ones he found interesting. He also made up many of his best: Bumble, Sowerberry, Sikes, Sally Thingummy, Fang, Chitling, Grimwig, Corney, Brittles, and Limbkins—all from *Oliver Twist*. And if he liked a name and it fit his character, he used it regardless. Thus, in *Oliver Twist*, he ironically named one of his villains Fagin—in spite of the real Bob Fagin's kindness to him at the bootblack factory. He paid great attention to how his words sounded. As a result, in a day when so many people still could not read or write, people loved listening to Dickens' words being read aloud, and Dickens would find a second career reading his own works to appreciative audiences.

In 1836, when Dickens was twenty-four, a group of his stories were published in a book titled *Sketches by Boz*. The book was so popular that a publisher suggested he write a novel to be published several chapters at a time in a monthly publication. Dickens accepted the challenge, leaving his reporting job behind to write it. He used a formula he would employ for his subsequent novels as well: producing two or three chapters at a time, always stopping at a point that would leave readers wanting to know what was about to happen and eager to buy the next issue to find out—a formula that would be used successfully from then on, not only by other writers of books and stories, but into the next century by radio and television soap operas.

This first novel, which he called *The Pickwick Papers,* was published in nineteen installments in 1836 and 1837. It was about a group of gentlemen, all members of the Pickwick Club, and their various adventures and adversities, and the ridiculous situations they got into. In one adventure they traveled to Rochester, the market town Dickens knew so well from his childhood, and stayed at the local inn. Dickens even managed to have Mr. Pickwick, the kind and charitable central character, wrongly sentenced to the notorious Fleet Prison because of an evil lawyer.

The Pickwick Papers found fans of all ages and all classes. One reviewer declared that the soul of Hogarth, England's most famous artist, had migrated into the body of Charles Dickens.

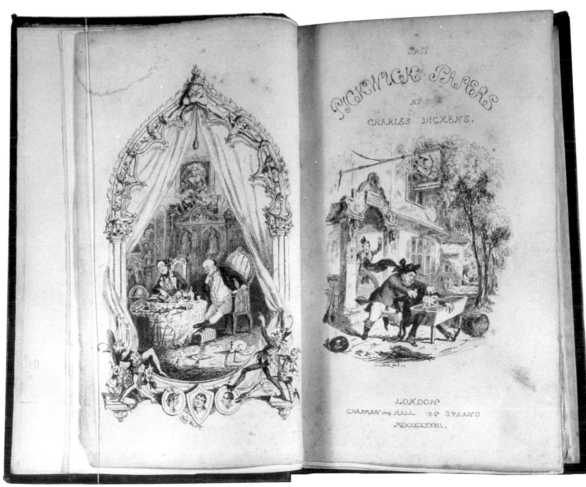

Dickens used his eye for detail to describe characters in depth and his ear for dialogue to have them engage in numerous conversations. Through all of it ran a vein of humor that had readers laughing out loud.

Londoners loved *The Pickwick Papers.* To Dickens' amazed delight, readers were of every class. The highborn read it in the comfort of their elegant homes or private clubs, and the poorest pooled their pennies to buy a copy of each periodical and found someone to read it to them. So popular was the series that it was immediately reprinted in American newspapers—though Dickens received no pay for this pirating of his work. Later novels would be much darker, but *Pickwick* was mostly lighthearted and often funny. When its run in the newspaper was finished, it came out in book form and sold very well.

Dickens' first novel made the former working-class boy the toast of London. He was just twenty-five years old.

Chapter 7

The Workhouse

PICKWICK'S SUCCESS GAVE Charles Dickens a loyal following and the confidence to write about his passion for the welfare of the poor.

No matter how many coins he gave to ragamuffin children on the streets of London, their lives could not improve until basic conditions changed for them. Working children were of special concern to Dickens. In his travels as a reporter, he had realized that his life as a bootblack boy had been easy compared to the harsh conditions imposed on armies of children employed in mills and factories all over the country.

Dickens also wanted to call attention to the workhouses. He had painful memories of his mother being faced with the choice of moving herself and the younger children into the workhouse or into John Dickens' small prison cell—and choosing prison because the workhouses were so much worse. They had been a British institution for centuries, and hundreds were scattered throughout the country, housing the elderly, sickly, disabled, and mentally ill. The many children living in them were usually orphaned or had been abandoned. The workhouses were meant to offer shelter to those who couldn't work—yet inmates were *expected* to work, if at all possible, to offset the cost of their care.

The New Poor Law, passed in 1834—ironically the same year the British colonies abolished slavery—left workhouse inmates little better off than slaves, where they lived in misery and were forced, if they could do any work at all, to labor for their keep. Authorities wanted to be sure that no one went to the workhouse until they had to. Otherwise, they reasoned, the poor might choose the workhouse over work. How could the rich stay rich and get richer if not for the cheap labor of the poor?

Workhouse officials were often corrupt, pocketing whatever they could from the funds paid by the parish for the care of inmates. Well-run workhouses where administrators were honest and inmates were treated well were the exception. Most were so awful that rather than go there, some people committed suicide or took their chances on the streets.

In an essay titled "A Walk in a Workhouse," Dickens wrote, "I walked . . . that Sunday morning through the little world of poverty enclosed within the workhouse walls. It was inhabited by a population of some fifteen-hundred or two thousand paupers, ranging from the infant newly born . . . to the old man dying on his bed." He saw "groves of babies in arms; groves of mothers and other sick women in bed; groves of lunatics; jungles of men in stone-paved downstairs day-rooms, waiting for their dinners; long and longer groves of old people, in upstairs infirmary wards, wearing out life, God knows how."

Dickens was deeply touched by the sight of a child who had just died. The little girl was referred to as "the dropped child" because she had been abandoned on the streets, "dropped" there, presumably by a family member. Dickens captured the humanity of the ward nurse, herself one of the inmates, who lamented the child, crying, "the dear, the pretty dear!" He added, with a Victorian flourish, "The dropped child seemed too small

Men and women ate separately in workhouses. These women are eating their sparse rations at London's Saint Pancras workhouse.

and poor a thing for Death to be earnest with, but Death had taken it . . . I heard a voice from Heaven saying, 'It shall be well for thee, Child.'"

To keep inmates uncomfortable and to constantly remind them of their low status, they were not allowed to have any personal possessions. They wore uniforms made from rough, stiff cloth and had their hair cut very short to help prevent lice. The sparse workhouse diet was mainly cheese, potatoes, bread, and an occasional bit of meat. It also included gruel, which was like thin, watery oatmeal. In some workhouses inmates actually got hot tea every day, but fruits, vegetables, sweets, and coffee were the rarest of treats.

Families who entered the workhouse were split up, with men, women, girls, and boys all assigned to separate dormitories. In some workhouses they were forbidden to speak to each other.

Young women who were pregnant and unmarried often ended up in the workhouse because they had nowhere else to go to deliver their babies. Two weeks after giving birth, they had a decision to make: they could either leave with their infants or stay. If they left, they took their chances on the streets. If they stayed, they had to go to work. Their babies were put in the workhouse nursery and cared for by elderly inmates, or sent away to "baby farms"—a form of foster care for infants and toddlers. Either way, children received little care. An observer wrote that the workhouse nursery was "often found under the charge of a person actually certified as of unsound mind, the bottles sour, the babies wet, cold and dirty." In many workhouses, the infant mortality rate was close to one hundred percent.

Still, children made up a third to half of the workhouse

population. Many impoverished mothers who could not feed their children had to put them there. Other child inmates were orphans or had been abandoned. They were given a bit of schooling and then put to work. Both boys and girls went into the factories or mills or did other kinds of hard labor. Others were hired out to farmers or shopkeepers. Some boys became chimney sweeps. Girls were often hired out to do menial chores in the homes of the middle class—like the workhouse girl who lived with Dickens' family for several years. It's possible Dickens learned enough from her about the workhouse to know that his mother made the right decision to move into the Marshalsea Prison.

Elderly women were often the caregivers for small children whose impoverished mothers had to work. In the workhouse system, the majority of these children died.

Emmeline Pankhurst, famous in England for helping women get the right to vote, wrote of visiting a workhouse: "I was horrified to see little girls seven and eight years old on their knees scrubbing the cold stones of the long corridors. These little girls were clad, summer and winter, in thin cotton frocks, low in the neck and short sleeved. . . . The fact that bronchitis was epidemic among them most of the time had not suggested to the guardians any change in the fashion of their clothes."

Dickens bristled at the injustice of the system. A story in the news at that time reported an inquiry into the deaths of a number of workhouse children. How could anyone—even someone who thought that the poor deserved to be poor—be indifferent to that? And yet people were.

He was thinking about writing a series of articles about the poor, but when he created a fictional sketch about a boy he called Oliver Twist, he saw the story's possibilities and began a novel. He wrote at white heat, spilling words onto paper, employing the elements of melodrama and pathos that were popular at the time. All through the story he exposed the injustices and harshness of the English class system on the poor—especially on children—and the indifference of the rich to their plight. He did not hold back in revealing the dark side of life: abuse of children, betrayal, murder, corruption, and filth figured in to his novel's complicated plot. He was determined to make the story so compelling that even if people found it distasteful, they would read it anyway. Dickens knew what it was like to have someone else controlling your life, and to be impoverished, miserable, and hungry. Through his main character, readers would know as well.

And who was Oliver Twist?

The lowest of the low: a workhouse orphan.

Chapter 8

Oliver Twist

THE NOVEL BEGAN ONE FATEFUL night in a workhouse near London when a mysterious, beautiful young woman gave birth, then said in a faint voice, "Let me see the child and die." The doctor attending her hesitated, but she stretched a weak hand toward her baby, and the doctor placed him in her arms. With her remaining strength, she kissed his forehead, then fell back and died.

An old woman, bleary from drinking beer, was the only other person in the shabby little room. The doctor asked if she knew anything about the baby's mother. The old woman could say only, "She was brought here last night. . . . She was found lying in the street; she had walked some distance, for her shoes were worn to pieces; but where she came from, or where she was going to, nobody knows."

The doctor lifted the cold left hand of the young woman who lay dead in the bed and saw that it had no wedding ring. "The old story," he said, shaking his head. And then he left.

As the old woman wrapped the baby in a dirty quilt, "Oliver cried lustily. If he could have known that he was an orphan, left to the tender mercies of church wardens and overseers, perhaps he would have cried the louder."

Because Oliver had no known relatives, "the workhouse authorities magnanimously and humanely resolved, that Oliver should be 'farmed,' or, in other words, that he should be dispatched to a branch-workhouse some three miles off, where twenty or thirty other juvenile offenders against the poor-laws rolled about the floor all day, without the inconvenience of too much food, or too much clothing, under the parental superintendence of an elderly female."

At the branch-workhouse, the caretaker hired by the parish to look after the children was "a woman of wisdom and experience; she knew what was good for children, and she had a very accurate perception of what was good for herself. So, she appropriated the greater part of the weekly stipend to her own use."

Though most of the other children died, Oliver somehow made it to his eighth birthday, an event that "found him a pale, thin child, somewhat diminutive in stature, and decidedly small in circumference. But nature or inheritance had implanted a good sturdy spirit in Oliver's breast; it had had plenty of room to expand, thanks to the spare diet of the establishment." He was taken back to his original workhouse, where the governing board informed him, "You have come here to be educated, and taught a useful trade." He was told that at six the next morning, he would begin the work of fraying old rope. He was shown to a rough, hard bed in a large ward, where he sobbed himself to sleep. Charles Dickens wrote, "What an illustration of the tender laws of this favored country! They let the paupers go to sleep!"

Because they were given so little food, Oliver and the other boys were very hungry and could finally stand it no more. "A council was held; lots were cast who should walk up to the master after supper that evening, and ask for more; and it fell to Oliver Twist."

At supper, as they finished their thin gruel, "the boys whispered to each other and winked at Oliver, while his next neighbors nudged him. Child as he was, he was desperate with hunger and reckless with misery. He rose from the table, and advancing, bowl and spoon in hand, to the master, said, somewhat alarmed at his own temerity—

George Cruikshank

Oliver asks for more in this famous scene from Oliver Twist. The artist who illustrated the first edition, George Cruikshank, also illustrated several other Dickens novels.

"'Please, sir, I want some more.'

"The master was a fat, healthy man, but he turned very pale. He gazed in stupefied astonishment on the small rebel for some seconds, and then clung for support to the copper. The assistants were paralyzed with wonder, and the boys with fear.

"'What!' said the master at length, in a faint voice.

"'Please, sir,' replied Oliver, 'I want some more.'"

For his impudence, Oliver found himself confined to a cold dark cell, while a sign was posted outside the workhouse offering a small reward to anyone who would take him as an apprentice. A master chimney sweep, who had already "bruised three or four boys to death," saw the notice and wanted Oliver, who was small and slim enough to get up the tightest chimney.

Odds were that Oliver would not have survived as a sweep. Through a stroke of luck, he was instead apprenticed to an undertaker, where he endured more mistreatment. When he went with his new master to a horrible slum to fetch the corpse of a mother who had starved to death, Charles Dickens did not spare his readers from the realities of this family's life. He also described the hovels that served as homes for the poor as "stagnant and filthy," where even the rats were "hideous with famine."

Oliver finally ran away, making his way toward London, a distance of seventy miles. While on the road, he met a boy known as the Artful Dodger, who fed him, for Oliver was starving, and offered to help him find work and lodgings in

London. They entered the city at night: "A dirtier or more wretched place [Oliver] had never seen. The street was very narrow and muddy, and the air was impregnated with filthy odors. There were a good many small shops; but the only stock in trade appeared to be heaps of children, who, even at that time of night, were crawling in and out at the doors, or scream-ing from the inside."

Thus began Oliver's adventures and misadven-tures in London. Along the way, Dickens exposed the workhouse system, corrupt public officials, children driven to crime to sup-port themselves, and the contrasts between the lives of the rich and poor. At the end of the long novel, after endless abuses, coin-cidences, close calls, evil acts, deceit, murder, and revelations, Oliver learned,

Dickens used an actual place, Field Lane, as the location for part of Oliver's adventures in London. Fagin's house was set in this crowded, high-crime slum, as were other scenes in the novel.

in fairy-tale fashion, that he was the son of a gentleman, now dead, and would inherit a fortune. He was reunited with his birth mother's sister, and after his adoption by his father's closest friend, he lived near this aunt and everyone was "truly happy."

Just like *The Pickwick Papers, Oliver Twist* came out in monthly installments. *Pickwick* had sold very well, but *Oliver Twist*

Oliver watches the Artful Dodger, a skillful pickpocket, at work in this scene from the novel. Oliver Twist *helped focus public attention on why so many children resorted to crime to support themselves.*

became a literary sensation. The public loved the story of the workhouse orphan and the travails he suffered at the hands of an uncaring world. Each publication day, people lined up to get the latest installment. The story also had devoted audiences in Europe and in America, where publishers once again pirated it, paying Dickens nothing.

Though the story is about the endearing, lovable Oliver, Dickens' objectives were clear: the novel exposed the appalling conditions of the workhouse, the exploitation of helpless children, society's indifference to the poor, and the ghastly slums that were breeding grounds for much of the city's violence and crime. That Dickens brought all of this to light in one novel was a remarkable feat. He also broke new literary ground, for *Oliver Twist* was the first English novel to have a child as its main character.

Some critics said that Dickens "sold out" by making Oliver highborn instead of lowborn. But Dickens knew he needed to engage the attention and sympathies of the upper classes. Through his powers as a storyteller, he made Oliver likable and sympathetic. Once his well-off readers began to truly care about Oliver, even though they believed him to be of lowly birth, Dickens revealed the workhouse orphan to be one of them. As a child, Dickens had accepted what he had been taught—that the poor were undeserving. When he became one of them, he learned that the poor had the very same hopes, fears, and feelings as the upper classes. With

Oliver Twist, his well-to-do readers learned this too.

The London Times, crusading for reform of the New Poor Law, reprinted the passage wherein Oliver begs, "Please, sir, I want some more," and included stories of terrible abuses in the workhouses. Dickens was thrust into the public spotlight as a spokesman championing the rights of the deserving poor. Along with speaking invitations came requests for interviews.

The boy who had been denied a formal education, who had worked as a common laborer in a blacking factory while his father was in prison, who had known hunger and want and had felt deserted by the world, was now recognized wherever he went, and was stopped on the streets by adoring fans requesting his autograph.

Not everyone loved *Oliver Twist.* Queen Victoria's prime minister, Lord Melbourne, told her after he'd read it, "It's all among workhouses, and coffin makers, and pickpockets . . . I don't *like* those things; I wish to avoid them; I don't like them in reality, and therefore I don't wish them represented."

But the queen said she found it "excessively interesting" and became one of Dickens' devoted fans, even if she wasn't particularly interested in assisting the poor. It would take more than one Dickens novel to help compel British society to create social reform, but it was *Oliver Twist,* published in 1838 when Dickens was only twenty-six, that set it all in motion.

Chapter 9

The Sea Captain Who Rescued Foundling Children

WHEN CHARLES DICKENS was twenty-five, he married his publisher's pretty daughter, Catherine, who was twenty. She was sweet natured and adored her handsome, ambitious, high-energy husband. Because of Dickens' success, he was soon able to buy them a proper home—a four-story townhouse in London's Bloomsbury neighborhood.

The first home Dickens purchased in London is now the Charles Dickens Museum. Visitors can learn about Dickens' family life and see the study where he wrote several of his novels.

To others it looked like his struggles were over, for he lived the life of a young gentleman. But even with money in his pocket and his growing fame, Dickens still saw himself in every ragged child who begged for a penny or slept in a doorway.

And what about helpless babies? As Dickens had related so movingly in *Oliver Twist,* only a few in the workhouses managed to survive childhood. A century earlier they could have been legally "dropped" as infants on the street—and none survived that. In response to this barbarity, a charity arose in the 1700s to provide a home for babies who might otherwise have met this fate. Called the London Foundling Hospital, it would benefit from Charles Dickens in many ways.

A "foundling" was a child whose parents were unknown, and "hospital" meant shelter. The Foundling Hospital was very much a shelter, but most of the children who grew up there were legally surrendered by a parent, rather than "found" somewhere. When Dickens moved to Bloomsbury, he was immediately drawn to the Foundling Hospital, an imposing red-brick institution located just four blocks from his new residence. It had been in operation for a hundred years and would be in operation another hundred, caring for a total of 27,000 foundlings, rearing them to be solid working-class citizens. At any given time, it housed 500 children.

Dickens and Catherine became patrons of the Foundling, sponsoring a pew in its chapel and attending Sunday services there. When Dickens learned about the old sea captain who had started this home for destitute children, and further learned the stories of two of its greatest patrons, he must have shivered with delight, for even he, the master story-teller, could not have created more appealing characters.

It all started with Thomas Coram, born in England in 1668 and sent to sea at age eleven after the death of his mother. Coram had a long career as a sailor and shipbuilder, lived for a time in America, and then settled with his American wife in London in 1722 when he was fifty-four years old.

Coram was a small, feisty man with a big personality. He loved children, though he had none of his own. Like Charles Dickens, he was restless, full of energy, and quick to help the less fortunate. Also like Dickens, he took long daily walks through the city.

As filthy as London was in Dickens' time, it was just as awful in Coram's. Even worse, every day the little sea captain came upon the bodies of dead and dying infants who had been "dropped" onto the streets to die a "natural" death. Murder was a

Hogarth's full-length portrait of Captain Coram hangs today in a place of honor in London's Foundling Museum.

capital offense in England, and mothers could be executed for such a crime—many were, in fact. But according to the law, "dropping" did not constitute murder.

Coram was sickened at the suffering of these children. Were the mothers monsters? Yet he knew that most of them were simply too poor to care for their babies and didn't know what else to do. If they were unmarried, they were looked down on by the middle and upper classes and denied work opportunities. Coram couldn't change that thinking, but he was determined to try to save as many of the children as he could by giving the mothers an alternative to abandoning them.

His vision was to create a home for the children. It wasn't realistic to think that anyone would adopt them—the upper classes weren't about to because of the class difference, and the lower classes couldn't afford to. So this would be the children's permanent home, where they would grow to young adulthood and then make their way into the world, prepared to support themselves and to be good citizens.

But who would pay for this home? If the church or government got involved, Coram knew they would demand control. He decided that funding must come from private sources—from wealthy, charitable individuals referred to in English society as the "Great and the Good."

To get their support, there had to be something in it for them, since they had little or no interest in the poor. Coram had an idea. England always needed sailors and soldiers to fight the country's never-ending wars. At the same time, the upper classes experienced a chronic shortage of well-trained servants. Therefore, Coram deemed, the boys would be trained for the military and the girls for domestic service.

To create a charity that could solicit contributions, Coram needed a Royal Charter from the king, for which he must present a petition signed by the Great and the Good. He set to work, walking long miles every day to visit these men, requesting their support. But most turned him down, so Coram turned to their wives, reasoning that the women were more likely to sympathize with the poor mothers who couldn't care for their babies. This produced an impressive number of signatures, but the biases against the poor were so strong that it still took Coram an incredible *seventeen* years to gather all the signatures he needed. The final one was his own. In 1739, when Coram was seventy-one years old, King George II granted him a Royal Charter for his "Hospital for the Maintenance and Education of Exposed and Deserted Young Children."

On his way at last, Coram selected a board of governors composed of influential members of the Great and the Good. They posted a notice that thirty infants no older than two months and free of contagious disease would be accepted, no questions asked, beginning at eight p.m., March 24, 1741. Anxious mothers holding infants gathered hours before the appointed time. Most wore the clothing of servants or poorly paid workers. The evening was emotional for everyone. Once the thirtieth child was accepted, the crowd was sent away. A report stated that the grief expressed by the mothers leaving their babies equaled that of the mothers whose children were not selected, and that altogether, "a more moving scene can't well be imagined."

Surprised at this response, the Great and the Good upped their pledges of support and over time the Foundling Hospital

After services in the Foundling chapel, members of the Great and the Good liked to watch the children eat their Sunday lunch. No one asked the children if this made them uncomfortable.

grew to be one of London's most fashionable charities. It would care for foundling children for the next 210 years.

In 1745 the Foundling Hospital moved into its new building on fifty-six acres of land. It could house 250 boys and 250 girls. It had several elegant rooms for use by the governors and the Great and the Good—an enticement to them to continue their involvement with the Foundling. The outside courtyard became a favored spot where wealthy Londoners came to walk or to ride in their carriages so they could see and be seen.

In the beginning the governors followed strict admission policies. Babies whose mothers bypassed these procedures and left them at the gate were taken to the workhouse, where they invariably perished.

So many mothers applied to leave their infants that the governors devised a lottery system. Whenever the Foundling announced openings, the Great and the Good assembled to watch as each desperate mother reached into a cloth bag and pulled out a colored ball. A black one meant she and her baby had to leave immediately. If white, the baby was accepted, provided it passed the health examination. A red ball meant the baby was put on a waiting list. During the first five years the lottery system was used, 2,500 mothers drew a ball from the bag and 763 of them left their babies at the Foundling.

The sprawling facility was always full, and money was a constant problem. In 1756, Parliament agreed to help, but required that all infants brought to the Foundling be admitted.

Mothers could place babies in a basket at the front gate at any time of the day or night, then ring the bell to notify the porter, and quickly disappear. The first night of this new system, the bell rang 117 times. By the end of the first month, the staff was overwhelmed trying to care for 425 new babies.

Each mother was required to leave an identifying token in the event that she wanted to one day reclaim her child. If she could write, she might leave a note or letter. Some were heartbreaking. One mother wrote, "Go gentle babe, and all thy life be happiness and love." Another left a silk purse, another a tiny fish carved of ivory. Others left lockets, ribbons, coins, rings or other jewelry. Staff carefully filed these items. The children never knew of their existence—and only a few mothers ever came back. Charles Dickens would later write a fictional story about one such mother who reclaimed her child.

During the four years that the Foundling had an open admission policy, it received more than 15,000 babies. They were from all over the country and included children with profound disabilities whose care further strained the Foundling's limited resources.

To stop this flood, the governors again changed the policy and now required mothers to submit to a traumatic interview. Many were servant girls who risked losing their desperately needed jobs since no self-respecting household would employ an unmarried servant with a child. These girls, often already devastated at parting with their babies, had to stand before the governors and state the father's name and occupation. It was well known that many of them had been impregnated against their will by the master of the house. But to remain employed, they had to name someone else. Could even Dickens have ever imagined a more excruciating scene?

If the governors agreed to take the baby, the mother was required to sever all contact: there would be no identifying tokens left this time. Even though a few mothers tried later to reclaim their children, most were denied, for the governors felt that the Foundling could do a better job raising the child than could a "tainted" parent.

To ensure their good health, Foundling children spent their first five years with a working-class nursing mother and her family in the countryside. Believing them to be their actual families, the children were frantic and heartbroken when they were taken from them and returned to the Foundling. Some of the families asked to adopt the children they had come to love, but just as with the birth mothers, the governors felt that the hospital's care was superior to what a lower-class family could offer.

Life at the Foundling was one of regimentation. The children could speak only when spoken to. Boys and girls were kept apart, even at mealtime, where they had to sit silent and still, eat every bite of food on their plates, and, on signal, start and stop at the same moment. Food was wholesome, but it was never plentiful and consisted of a few items served over and over again. One foundling said, "We were always hungry!"

Girls wore identical uniforms, and so did boys. All clothing was shared communally, and both boys and girls learned to mend clothing and darn socks. Children slept two to a bed, fifty to a ward. Older children helped the younger ones with bathing and dressing. Daytime was carefully scheduled with work, school, and outdoor exercise.

Both boys and girls received a basic education, then most boys went into the military, while the girls were trained to be

Foundling children are at work on their studies in this photo taken in 1941 during the Foundling's final decade.

household servants, just as Captain Coram first envisioned. Few of the children aspired to anything else. "We weren't going to be wonderful," one girl said. "We were mostly going into service."

At a time when abandoned and orphaned children often starved or froze to death on the streets or perished in the workhouses, and when children younger than ten accounted for half of the deaths in London, Foundling children were clean, fed, and safe. They had medical care and were educated for a trade. By age fourteen, most had already been apprenticed as servants or had entered the military. In many ways they were the most fortunate of underprivileged children. The Foundling's goal of raising them to be solid citizens was largely successful.

But Charles Dickens would have realized that the children's emotional lives were mostly ignored, just as he felt his own had been by his mother and father. Founding children received little affection from staff. One woman raised by the Foundling said there were no good-night hugs or kisses, or any comfort given to crying children. They were constantly reminded that they must be grateful for the care they received. They understood vaguely that they had no mothers or fathers because something bad had happened and that they were somehow to blame. As they grew older, many suffered from anxiety and depression. One said, "We were guilty and we *felt* guilty, and . . . that guilt follows you through life—it doesn't disappear. . . . I'm a grown man, but it still goes through my mind, the guilt."

As adults, most expressed gratitude to the Foundling for their upbringing. Yet many struggled to lead normal lives or to marry and parent children of their own, choosing instead to remain in the military or in domestic service. Others wanted families more than anything and became devoted spouses and parents.

Not long after the Foundling opened, the old sea captain, Thomas Coram, was ousted by the board of governors after he apparently said something that offended several of them. In spite of this, when he died in 1751 at the age of eighty-four, his funeral was held in the Foundling Hospital's chapel. It was attended by the governors and many dignitaries who praised the humble man who saw a problem and through pure grit created a solution that saved the lives of destitute children.

A century later, his example would inspire England's greatest author, Charles Dickens.

Chapter 10

The Great Benefactors: Handel, Hogarth, and Dickens

THE CHAPEL AT THE FOUNDLING HOSPITAL was always full for Sunday services. Dressed in their best clothes, Charles Dickens and his wife, Catherine, took their places in their private pew and gazed around at Londoners from all walks of life who came so they could hear the children's choir. Many were moved to tears whenever the children sang "Blessed Are They That Considereth the Poor," the song known as the Foundling Hospital anthem.

It was a source of pride for all of London that this song had been composed specifically for the Foundling children by the great German composer George Frideric Handel, who had lived much of his life in London and had become a British citizen. In fact, Handel, one of the most famous men of his time, had served on the Foundling's board of governors,

Handel was given the high honor of burial in Westminster Abbey's Poet's Corner. German by birth, he is often referred to as a German-born English composer.

and his masterpiece, *Messiah,* came to be closely associated with the Foundling.

Like the sea captain Thomas Coram, Handel could have been Dickens' creation. He was a big, heavy man, sometimes called "the great bear." He dressed stylishly and wore an elaborate wig with long cascading curls. This, along with his size, made him immediately recognizable to Londoners. He spoke with a thick German accent and when he got angry he swore loudly, his words tumbling together in German, English, and Italian. As much as he loved children, he did not marry and had none of his own.

Handel lived a century before Dickens. But if the composer and the author had known each other, they might have been fast friends, for in addition to their many accomplishments, both were charitable by nature, especially when it came to helping underprivileged children.

Handel was born in 1685 in Halle, Germany. Like the English, the Germans loved music and honored musicians—but paid them very little. Handel showed unusual musical ability as a child, but his father was determined that he not grow up to be a poor musician. According to a story that may or may not be true, Handel's mother smuggled a harpsichord—an instrument rather like a miniature piano—into the attic of the family home and covered the strings to muffle sound. At night, when his father was asleep, Handel went to the attic and taught himself to play. At some point his father found out and finally allowed his son to study music.

While mastering the organ, harpsichord, and violin, Handel also wrote music. To please his practical father he went to law school, but in his spare time he worked on his compositions and served as a church organist. When he began earning money from music, he dropped law and went to Italy to study opera. In 1712—exactly one hundred years before Dickens was born—twenty-six-year-old Handel moved to London, where he enjoyed great popularity as a composer and a performer.

Money was often an issue, even for such a famous composer, but Handel was always generous to the less fortunate. He sometimes donated all concert proceeds to charity. A frequent recipient was the Fund for the Support of Decayed Musicians and their Families. Proceeds from a benefit concert in Dublin freed 142 men from debtors' prison. It's been said of Handel that no other composer ever contributed so much to the relief of human suffering.

In 1749, when he learned that the four-year-old Foundling Hospital needed funds to complete its chapel, he offered to

This painting, circa 1740, of Handel conducting Messiah *shows him wearing the elaborate wig and clothing favored by upper-class men at that time.*

hold a charity concert, presenting a new composition that he called, simply, *Messiah*. The Foundling's governors were delighted, knowing that Handel always drew huge crowds. To create as much space as possible, they requested that ladies not wear hoop skirts and that gentlemen leave their swords at home.

More than a thousand people attended the concert in the unfinished chapel. So many others were turned away that

This painting, circa 1740, of Handel conducting Messiah *shows him wearing the elaborate wig and clothing favored by upper-class men at that time.*

Handel immediately scheduled a second performance, and enough money was raised to finish the chapel. *Messiah*, which relates in song the story of Jesus Christ's death and resurrection, went on to become Handel's most famous composition. When the king attended one of the performances, he stood during the "Hallelujah Chorus" and audiences have been standing for it ever since.

After that first concert, the Foundling Hospital and *Messiah* enjoyed a fruitful partnership. Until his death a decade later, Handel himself directed

Messiah at the Foundling chapel at least once a year, always to overflow crowds. These benefit performances raised a sum that today would equal $1.5 million and helped stabilize the Foundling's finances. Even after Handel's death, the concerts continued as an annual event—part of the composer's legacy to the Foundling's children. It's very possible that Dickens and his family attended at least one.

In 1750 Handel became one of the hospital's governors. Because of him, music became part of the children's education. Every child age nine and up sang in the choir or played an instrument. The Foundling also had a highly regarded boys' band—which Dickens would one day write about. Handel donated a fine organ for the chapel, personally overseeing its design and construction, and playing it himself on a number of occasions. It's thought that he even accompanied the children a few times as they sang the anthem he composed for them.

He might have become even more involved with the children, but his health deteriorated. When he could no longer conduct *Messiah*, he still attended its performances at the Foundling Hospital. He did so until two weeks before his death in 1759 at age seventy-four. In his will he bequeathed one of the priceless, original copies of *Messiah* to the Foundling.

Services for Handel at London's great cathedral, Westminster Abbey, drew three thousand mourners. He was laid to rest in the floor of the Abbey's famed Poet's Corner. More than a century later, in 1870, another famous Londoner with ties to the

Foundling Hospital would be interred next to him: the novelist Charles Dickens.

Hogarth's self-portrait painted in 1758 reveals that he dressed simply and refused to wear a wig, which he considered pretentious.

While Handel was the most famous composer of his day, his contemporary William Hogarth was the most famous artist. Like Handel, he had a close relationship with the Foundling Hospital. And while the Foundling children grew up with music because of Handel, they grew up surrounded by art because of Hogarth.

The artist was born in London in 1697. Just as Charles Dickens would later sketch what he saw with words, Hogarth sketched with pencil and paper. The two men shared another link: both had loving fathers who ended up in debtors' prison. Hogarth was ten when he and his two sisters and mother moved with Hogarth's father to the wretched Fleet Prison (which Dickens' novel *Pickwick*

Papers is often credited with helping to close). Hogarth never talked of the four years his family spent there, but it had a profound impact on him and on his art, instilling in him a lifelong disdain for the upper classes, a hatred of hypocrisy, and a quickness to defend the innocent.

Unlike the great bear Handel, Hogarth was physically small—about five foot in height. He was very intelligent, and always opinionated and outspoken. He was also handsome, with bright eyes and great energy. Wigs were the style of the day—Handel's was enormous—but Hogarth never wore one, considering them pretentious. Like Coram, Hogarth married but had no children. And like Coram, Handel, and later Dickens, he loved children. He often placed both children and animals in his work. Society typically viewed children as miniature adults, but Hogarth saw them as so much more, and he was known for his sensitivity in capturing their joyous expressions.

He became a skilled engraver and then a self-taught artist. Before long, he gained acclaim for his topical satire and biting humor, poking fun at self-important people. At the time, only one out of two people could read, but everyone could look at Hogarth's prints and understand his message. Because the target of his satire was occasionally undeserving rich people, the deserving poor loved him—though he sometimes ridiculed them too.

He satirized the upper classes, prisons, the military, politics, and election corruption—whatever social problem caught his attention. No one was spared. In one of his most famous prints he lashed out at the evil of alcohol at a time when gin was the national drink, consumed by both children and adults, and alcoholism was widespread. Titled *Gin Lane,* the print depicts a mother so drunk that her baby is slipping out of her arms and falling to its death. *Gin Lane* helped get legislation passed that placed restrictions on the sale of alcohol.

Hogarth filled his busy canvases with characters and stories. Dickens would study them a century later, learning how telling a small detail could be, and that a main plot could be enriched by dozens of supportive stories. That the artist dared satirize English society was also a strong influence on Dickens, who credited Hogarth as one of his inspirations for writing about "miserable reality" in *Oliver Twist.* He referred to Hogarth as "the moralist

Hogarth's depiction of alcoholism in this 1751 sketch inspired laws to limit the sale of alcohol.

and censor of his age," who possessed "a power and depth of thought which belonged to few men before him, and will probably appertain to fewer still in time to come."

Hogarth was middle-aged when he began his involvement with Coram's Foundling Hospital. Like Handel, his famous name helped draw attention to the charity. He was one of its first governors and designed the Foundling Hospital seal, its coat of arms, and the children's brown and scarlet uniforms.

Like Handel, Hogarth wanted to find ways to ensure long-term financial support for the Foundling. Artists had nowhere to display their art where the wealthy might see it and buy it. So he started London's first art gallery at the Foundling, reasoning that art patrons would pay to see the art and then might be moved to contribute to the care of the children. Soon the Foundling became a gathering spot for artists, some of whom donated their paintings to the Foundling's permanent collection, including the famed artists Joshua Reynolds and Thomas Gainsborough.

Three of Hogarth's finest works were also part of the permanent collection, and today they hang in the Foundling Museum in London. They include *Moses Brought Before Pharaoh's Daughter*, which he painted specifically for the Foundling; *The March of the Guards to Finchley*, considered one of his best works; and finally his magnificent full-length portrait of Captain Thomas Coram.

Usually only the nobility and the very rich had their

portraits painted, especially by an artist as famous as Hogarth. And only prominent and important people had full-length portraits painted. But Hogarth didn't care. He admired the determined sea captain who had sacrificed so much to start the Foundling Hospital and asked Coram to pose for him. He said, "I painted with most pleasure," and he was convinced that the portrait was the best of all his work. Dickens would have known the painting well, for it had a place of honor at the Foundling Hospital. It revealed a cheerful, honest man. In the portrait Coram is seated in a chair and his short legs don't quite touch the floor (see page 65).

Today, in a city filled with great art, the collection at the Foundling remains one of the best in London. Because of Hogarth, artists and the Foundling Hospital are forever connected.

A century after Handel and Hogarth did so much to help the Foundling, Charles Dickens brought it new acclaim with his writing.

In 1853 he published an article titled "Received a Blank Child," taking its title from the first line of the Foundling's admission document that had blank spaces where officials filled out the date and gender of each baby being admitted. This document began: "The [blank] day of [blank], received a [blank] child." In his article, Dickens described the Foundling's impressive building and grounds and told of watching the children completing their lessons and being "trained out of their blank state to be useful entities in life." He concluded, "From what we have seen of this establishment we have derived much satisfaction."

He drew readers' attention to the Foundling again in his novel *Little Dorrit*, published in 1857. In it, he paid tribute to Thomas Coram in the naming of "Tattycoram," who was raised in the Foundling and became a servant in the home of the Meagles family. Mr. Meagles explained to a guest that his family always attended services at the Foundling chapel, and because they greatly admired Thomas Coram, in Coram's honor they added "coram" to Tatty's name. In *Oliver Twist*, Oliver's kind benefactor is named John Brownlow, a name borrowed from Dickens' friend John Brownlow, who grew up in the Foundling Hospital and served on its staff for almost sixty years.

Other mentions appeared in Dickens' writings in reference to place, as when he located an isolated tavern near the Foundling, or mentioned the sound of its bell. He wrote about the Foundling's famous boys' band. His story *No Thoroughfare* had several scenes set in the Foundling Hospital. Part of this story's plot was foreshadowed in *Little Dorrit* when Mr. and Mrs. Meagles attended Sunday chapel services there. While listening to the children's choir sing, Mrs. Meagles wondered, "Does any wretched mother ever come here, and look among those young faces, wondering which is the poor child she brought into this forlorn world, never through all its life to know her love, her kiss, her face, her voice, even her name!" In *No Thoroughfare*, a mother did indeed come to claim her son, years after anonymously leaving him at the Foundling.

Eventually the Foundling outgrew its mission. By the 1950s, children who in earlier years would have grown up at the Foundling were being placed with foster or adoptive families. The old building was torn down and the Foundling Hospital became known as the Coram Family. Today, Coram Family is a strong and vibrant organization that helps London's needy children. Its headquarters, a children's playground, and the Foundling Museum now occupy the site of the original Foundling Hospital.

Honoring the tradition of Hogarth and Handel, artists and musicians participate in concerts, exhibits, and workshops at the Foundling Museum to benefit Coram Family projects. One popular project each September is welcoming street children to the museum and exhibiting artwork inspired by them, alongside artwork created by them.

Every year the museum hosts an annual Handel concert. Visitors to the museum learn about the Foundling Hospital and Thomas Coram, and they view Hogarth's paintings and the museum's copy of Handel's *Messiah*. They also hear about the hospital's special friend Charles Dickens, who used his talent to do what Coram, Hogarth, and Handel used theirs for: to inspire people to get involved in the rescue and care of impoverished children.

Chapter 11

Closing England's Worst Schools

WHEN CHARLES DICKENS WAS a child living in the village of Chatham, he heard a ghastly story he never forgot. A local boy had been sent far away to a boarding school in the Yorkshire area of northern England. When he returned after many months, he had an oozy open sore on his cheek. It had started as something small but had become badly infected when the headmaster "ripped it open with an inky pen-knife" to drain puss from it, rather than send the boy to a doctor.

"The impression made on me never left me," Dickens wrote of this mistreatment. "I was always curious about Yorkshire schools." These cheap, isolated boarding schools, of which there were a couple dozen, were known to be places where boys were sent to live by indifferent parents or incompetent guardians who wanted them out of the way. Some actually

Classroom discipline in all schools could be harsh in Dickens' time, but conditions were so much worse in the Yorkshire boarding schools that Dickens was determined to close them.

advertised that students were allowed no vacations unless parents requested it. Going to one could be a death sentence.

Not even a highly publicized court case could close them. In 1823, parents of two boys who went blind from untreated infections sued their sons' headmaster, William Shaw. It was revealed during the trial that at Shaw's school the food often had maggots in it and an average of five boys had to share each flea-infested bed. The court found Shaw guilty of various charges. But his school stayed open, for the government had no control over education, and uncaring parents continued to send Shaw their defenseless sons.

As a schoolboy Dickens had seen plenty of mistreatment of students. Physical punishment was not questioned in a society that believed the dictum "spare the rod and spoil the child." Dickens felt it was criminal that men with little or no education could open schools and establish themselves as the headmasters and abuse their students. He wrote that his own headmaster at the last school he attended "was by far the most ignorant man I have ever had the pleasure to encounter and one of the worst-tempered men perhaps who ever lived." Dickens often saw that bad temper turned against his classmates, but it was nothing compared to the stories about the Yorkshire boarding schools.

Dickens learned from the public's embrace of *Oliver Twist* and the subsequent outcry against the workhouses how much power he wielded as a writer, and he was determined to use it to end the suffering of innocent boys by closing down the Yorkshire schools. These boys' parents might not care what happened to them, but Dickens did.

He began working on a story about a young man he named Nicholas Nickleby, who goes to teach in one of the Yorkshire schools, realizes the horrific conditions, confronts the brutal headmaster, and, after many twists and turns, gets the school shut down. *Nicholas Nickleby* would be his third novel.

To portray his fictional school accurately, Dickens wanted to visit several of the real schools. In January 1838, when he was twenty-six, he and a friend traveled from London to Yorkshire by horse-drawn coach—an exhausting trip of 240 miles that took several days over rough roads through snow and cold. When they arrived, Dickens began inquiring about boarding schools in the area, pretending that he was acting on behalf of a widow who was seeking a place to send her son.

Finding locals reluctant to talk, he went on his own to visit William Shaw's school. The notorious headmaster knew who Dickens was and was wary of him.

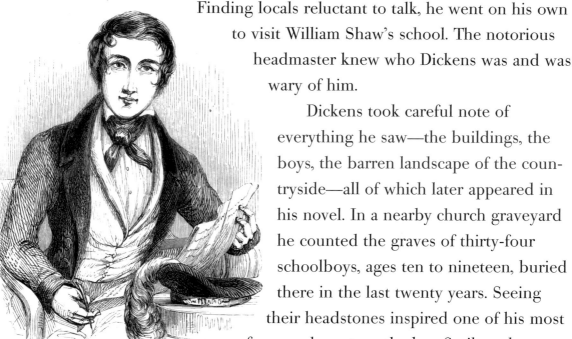

Dickens took careful note of everything he saw—the buildings, the boys, the barren landscape of the countryside—all of which later appeared in his novel. In a nearby church graveyard he counted the graves of thirty-four schoolboys, ages ten to nineteen, buried there in the last twenty years. Seeing their headstones inspired one of his most famous characters: the boy Smike, who dies in *Nicholas Nickleby* as the result of illness brought on by his mistreatment at Dickens' fictional school.

Dickens' hero, Nicholas Nickleby, is an intelligent and compassionate young man who is horrified by the ill treatment of students at the Yorkshire school where he is hired to teach.

Home from his journey, Dickens set to work. Once again he employed romance, comedy, pathos, and melodrama, along with a colorful cast of characters that included devilish villains, brave heroes, and virtuous heroines—all the things Victorian readers loved. He called his boarding school Dotheboys Hall. Its students—thin, pale, and fearful young boys—suffered the evils present in actual Yorkshire schools: squalid living conditions, vermin, illness, disease, beatings, and starvation.

Dickens wrote in the book's introduction that the Yorkshire headmasters were "the lowest and most rotten . . . traders in the avarice, indifference, or imbecility of parents, and the helplessness of children; ignorant, sordid, brutal men, to whom few considerate persons would have entrusted the board and lodging of a horse or dog." He created one of the most villainous of all headmasters in sadistic Wackford Squeers, an apelike man with one eye, whose trousers were too short, his sleeves too long, and with hair that stood on end. He had "a very sinister appearance, especially when he smiled, at which times his expression bordered closely on the villainous." Through threats, beatings, and starvation, Squeers kept the boys in his charge so terrified of him that they dared not complain.

When the novel was published in serial form in 1838 and 1839, it created a sensation. Several headmasters, including William Shaw, threatened Dickens with legal action, certain they were the model for Squeers. Nothing came of their threats, for Dickens had become too powerful a public figure to sue.

His response to his accusers was

Even though Dickens' villainous headmaster Wackford Squeers was a fictitious character, several Yorkshire head-masters tried to sue Dickens, saying Squeers was based on them.

to write, "Mr. Squeers is the representative of a class, and not of an individual. Where imposture, ignorance, and brutal cupidity are the stock in trade of a small body of men, and one is described by these characteristics, all his fellows will recognize something belonging to themselves, and each will have a misgiving that the portrait is his own."

Dickens had exposed the Yorkshire schools and his public heard him. Even the cruelest parents hurriedly withdrew their sons. Schools closed, and within a year, few were left. School inspection by the government did not begin in England until 1864, but the first commissioner to visit schools in the Yorkshire area reported that he "wholly failed to discover an example of the typical Yorkshire school with which Dickens had made us familiar." According to one Dickens biographer, the author had single-handedly eliminated "a national abuse."

Dickens found this quite satisfying. But more reform was badly needed. He pointed out "the monstrous neglect of education in England, and the disregard of it by the State." Half the population was illiterate, unable to afford the luxury of learning to read and write. The quality of a child's education depended on what parents could pay—and the poor could pay nothing. Dickens had a new cause to advance: radical though it seemed to the middle and upper classes, Dickens felt that slum children, too, had a right to an education. And that it should be free.

Chapter 12

Sending Ragged Children to School

THE UPPER CLASSES debated endlessly about educating the poor. If poor children learned to read, write, and do simple math, they had increased value as workers. But if they could read and began to learn, they might want to better themselves and would be less accepting of their dismal lot in life.

Thomas Guthrie, a popular Scottish minister, started the Ramsay Lane Ragged School in Edinburgh, where he helped teach the city's most destitute children.

Also, with the ability to communicate in writing, they might organize and—this was the real fear—rebel against those who had held them down for so long. The upper classes were only too aware of what had happened during the French Revolution in neighboring France: in 1789 the monarchy was toppled and the royal family and other wealthy aristocrats executed. Remembering this, the upper classes were of a mind to keep the lower classes ignorant.

Charles Dickens felt the opposite—that unless poor children were saved from a "doomed childhood," as he called it, they would one day rise up and tear down British society. Others shared this belief. One pioneer in education warned that the children of the poor would do no better than their parents unless "a helping hand is held out to the children to aid them to rise to a higher and better life." Reform was afoot in Queen Victoria's England, and it included education for the masses.

Because religion was important to many of the British, a few charity schools had long existed that tried to teach children to read the Bible. Most classes were held on Sundays, the only day laboring children could attend. One concern about these Sunday Schools came from police, some of whom were convinced that little thieves who could read would use this skill to compare price tags and then steal the more expensive item.

But even with strong objection from the upper classes, Ragged Schools gradually developed from the Sunday Schools, taking their name from the appearance of the boys and girls who attended them. Like Sunday Schools, Ragged Schools taught religion and reading, but also writing and math, along with training for jobs that would help children earn better livings than they could from hard labor.

In 1844, Lord Shaftesbury, a powerful member of Parliament, a dedicated reformer, and a great admirer of Dickens' writing, organized nineteen London schools into the Ragged Schools Union. Its goal was to reach the most needy slum children, including orphans and children whose parents either were in prison or were too drunk or too poor to care for them. Because of Lord Shaftesbury's influence, other prominent individuals and reformers got involved in starting schools. So did churches. At its peak, London's Ragged School Union had almost two hundred schools offering education to close to 50,000 children.

Finding locations children could get to meant that schools were often set up in old factories or warehouses located in or near the slums. Such buildings tended to be cold in winter and hot in summer. Because nearly all children had to work, classes were held in the evening and on weekends.

The volunteer teachers, who came from the middle and upper classes, were sincere in their desire to help, but many simply couldn't handle the challenges. Most classes were badly overcrowded. Teachers faced as many as two hundred students squeezed onto hard benches in a classroom that reeked of dirty bodies and unwashed clothing. The boys and girls came from a rough-and-tumble world and knew little about manners or polite behavior. They pushed, shoved, and yelled. Frequent fights broke out, and sometimes the police had to be called.

In spite of the obstacles, children poured in, aware that education offered them hope of a better life. A ten-year-old girl told how she worked as a "baby-minder" for twelve hours a day, except for the two days a week when she left an hour early so she could attend school. A boy who supported himself by finding and selling bits of metal said, "I go to a Ragged School three times a week if I can . . . I should like to know how to read."

Children had another motivation for coming to school. Officials quickly realized that boys and girls whose stomachs were rumbling from hunger had difficulty studying. Many of the schools found funding to offer both breakfast and dinner—often the only food a child might get that day. Most schools also provided clothing for the children, who even in wintertime might not have shoes, much less warm clothes.

The majority of teachers went out of their way to be kind to their students, knowing they struggled to come to school. Parents could be the biggest obstacle, demanding that their children stay home to care for younger siblings, or go out to work instead—just as Dickens' parents had. Some parents feared their children would think themselves to be better than them if they knew how to read and write. But there were also parents who made great sacrifices to get their children to school, and some even attended classes with their children in hopes of improving their own lot in life.

Dickens was a strong supporter of the Ragged Schools. Most of these schools included religious education as part of

Children receive a much-needed meal at the Lamb and Flag Ragged School in London in this 1849 illustration. Reformers quickly realized that children learned best—and were most likely to come to classes—if their stomachs were fed as well as their minds.

the curriculum, and Dickens was not comfortable with this. But he didn't protest, for he realized that religion allowed the children to "look forward . . . to another life, which would correct the miseries and woes of this."

His interest in educating slum children was "intense and prolonged," according to one historian. It began when Dickens visited a Ragged School operating in a rundown house in one of London's worst slums. Afterward, he wrote, "I have very seldom seen . . . anything so shocking as the dire neglect of soul and body exhibited in these children." The odor of the dirty children was so overpowering that the friend with him had to leave. Dickens stayed, talking to the boys and girls and watching them at their lessons.

In a lengthy letter to the editor of the *Daily News* he urged Londoners to visit Ragged Schools and see for themselves the good work taking place. "The name implies the purpose," he wrote. "They who are too ragged, wretched, filthy, and forlorn to enter any other place, who could gain admission into no charity school, and who would be driven from any church door, are invited to come in here, and find some people . . . willing to teach them something, and show them some sympathy, and stretch a hand out, which is not the iron hand of the Law."

He acknowledged that the Ragged School system was imperfect, but made clear his "appreciation of the efforts of these teachers [and] my true wish to promote them by any slight means in my power." Dickens persuaded a wealthy friend to assist the school he had visited. At his insistence, the improved quarters were equipped with water so the children could wash themselves—a radical notion for the times.

Dickens considered opening his own Ragged School and spoke of it often. He did not accomplish this, but he remained interested in the schools and often recommended to laboring children that they attend them.

He also urged the government to assist the schools, but even England's most famous author could not get *that* accomplished.

Dickens would have known of the work of Dr. Barnardo, whose name is linked to the Ragged Schools, though it is not known if the two men were friends. Thomas John Barnardo was a huge personality who could have stepped from one of Dickens' novels. Born in Dublin, Ireland, in 1845, he was brilliant, handsome, charming, argumentative, easily bored—and always well dressed. He was also a devout Christian who taught Bible classes in one of Dublin's Ragged Schools. He wanted to be a medical missionary in China and he came to London to study medicine. He chose to live in a poor area of the city so that along with his studies, he could teach the Bible in a Ragged School, just as he had in Dublin. When one of the boys in his class revealed that he slept outdoors, Dr. Barnardo refused to believe it. The boy showed him where he and many other

Thomas Barnardo, an Irish medical doctor, was a leading social reformer in London, where he cared for needy children. He is shown here in 1900, five years before his death at age sixty.

homeless children, some as young as six, huddled together through the night for warmth and protection. The young Irishman had seen abject poverty in Dublin, but this still shocked him.

When a cholera epidemic in 1866 killed thousands of Londoners, most of them in the slums and the majority of them children, Dr. Barnardo realized he was needed right there. He finished his medical studies and for the next forty years cared for London's "waifs and strays." His organization became known as the East End Juvenile Mission. A sign over one of its buildings read NO DESTITUTE CHILD EVER REFUSED ADMISSION.

Dr. Barnardo was a force to be reckoned with. He established a mission church and became a well-known preacher, converting many slum-dwellers to Christianity. He turned a former gin palace into a coffee bar, where he welcomed all ages, offering them coffee, tea, and hot chocolate. He took as many as five hundred Sunday School children by train on annual country outings, where they could play all day and enjoy picnic meals far away from the city's slums. As with his other programs, he paid for it entirely through charitable donations, for he was a master at fundraising. Many people who gave money to his causes had been inspired by the writings of Charles Dickens.

Dr. Barnardo married, and he and his wife had seven children. When one was born with Down's syndrome, Dr. Barnardo established a home for children with special needs. He also opened shelters for homeless children that became known as Dr. Barnardo Homes. He felt it was always better for children to grow up in families instead of institutions, so he started a program to board homeless children with foster families, eventually helping more than 2,000 children find homes. He also assisted 18,000 children in immigrating to other countries, where most did very well.

One of his Ragged Schools, London's largest with more than a thousand children enrolled, opened in a converted warehouse in 1877 on Copperfield Road, which was named for the title character of Charles Dickens' great novel *David Copperfield*. In the novel, the boy David Copperfield had to work in a factory—just like his creator, Charles Dickens, and just like many of the boys and girls attending Copperfield Road Ragged School.

In the wintertime, children at the school received both breakfast and dinner, for like others who ran Ragged Schools,

Dr. Barnardo understood the importance of feeding the children. He wrote, "They know what it is to have no fire in the grate and no bread in the cupboard. . . . We find in many cases that food is more essential to the boys and girls than education."

A heart condition worsened by overwork killed Dr. Barnardo when he was sixty. At the time, in addition to his Ragged Schools, he had ninety-six residential homes caring for nearly 10,000 children, many of them with disabilities. He is credited with rescuing at least 60,000 children from the streets, caring for and educating them, teaching them trades and helping them find jobs.

On the day of his funeral, flags were at half-staff and houses were draped in black. Tearful crowds filled the streets in the slums, bowing their heads in respect as the horse-drawn hearse bearing the doctor's coffin passed by.

It took until 1870, the year of Dickens' death, for England to institute compulsory education for all children five to thirteen years of age. The Ragged Schools were the forerunner of this national school system. They gave a basic education to slum children, turning them from street urchins into employable young people with the tools to escape the violence and poverty that had marked their lives.

Today the Copperfield Road Ragged School is the Ragged School Museum and welcomes visitors. Inside it looks much as

Dr. Barnardo started the Copperfield Road Ragged School in an old warehouse. It was London's largest free school and is today the Ragged School Museum, where visitors can sit in desks once occupied by children from nearby slums.

it did when children from the surrounding slums poured in to receive nourishment for their minds and bodies. Visitors learn about Dr. Barnardo and his quest to care for homeless children.

And they hear about Charles Dickens, whose writings helped bring about changes in society that improved the lives of poor children—some of whom learned their ABCs in a Ragged School located on a road named for one of Dickens' most beloved characters.

Chapter 13

Giving from a Charitable Heart

EVEN WHEN HE BECAME FAMOUS, Charles Dickens feared being unable to support his family. He suffered from flashbacks, remembering how he once labored long hours in the blacking factory and never knew if he would have enough to eat. He worried that something bad could happen—something he couldn't control—that would put him back on the streets, but this time with a wife and children to care for.

By the age of thirty-one, he had authored eight books, several of them bestsellers. He was the publisher and editor of a popular news magazine, to which he frequently contributed articles, and he was in constant demand as a speaker. But that year, 1843, he was especially concerned about money. He and Catherine had been married six years and were expecting their fifth child. Dickens' large household included servants, his wife's sister, and assorted pets. His father, perpetually in debt, always needed financial help, as did several of Dickens' brothers and sisters. Dickens gave generously to charities and was quick to help out friends. With so many bills to pay, Dickens was forced to borrow money again. If there was one thing he hated, it was debt.

As popular as he was, his last couple of books had brought in less income than he had counted on. He needed to produce something that could make money quickly.

Ideas tumbled in his mind. As always his concerns included the welfare of the lower classes, especially the children. He intended to continue exposing the greed and indifference of wealthy people who exploited the poor for their own benefit. Those with the most often gave the least, believing the poor should help themselves. Dickens wanted to change their feelings about the lower classes— to make them *want* to help the less fortunate. He also wanted to remind the upper classes that unless they supported social reforms to improve the lives of the poor, a rebellion like the French Revolution was very possible.

Gradually a story started to take shape in his mind. Excited, he realized that it would address his goals and still be highly entertaining, for he was envisioning a ghost story—and not just a story with one ghost, but with *three*. The Victorians were very interested in the paranormal. A ghost story was *just* the thing.

As soon as he started to write, he became so engaged in his creation that he was "reluctant to lay it aside for a moment" and found, "I was very much affected by the little Book myself." He worked nonstop, completing what he referred to as "this ghostly little book" in just six weeks.

He set it at Christmas, then a minor holiday in England. Once it had been an occasion of feasting and merriment. That had changed two centuries earlier when austere religious reformers had decreed through an act of Parliament that Christmas must be a somber occasion, marked by repentance of wrongdoing. But many people, including Dickens, still celebrated Christmas with a traditional dinner of roast goose, plum pudding, and mince pie, and with the long-held tradition of charitable giving to the poor.

Dickens called his lengthy short story *A Christmas Carol.* As was so often true in his books, a child played a pivotal role. Tiny Tim was a small boy slowly dying of what was possibly rickets, a crippling disease caused by a vitamin deficiency related to malnutrition.

The story opened with the words, "Marley was dead, to begin with." Marley was the former partner of Ebenezer Scrooge, "a squeezing, wrenching, grasping, scraping, clutching, covetous, old sinner! Hard and sharp as flint . . . and self-contained, and solitary as an oyster." Scrooge had grown rich by hoarding his earnings. He had no life outside of work. His only relative was his charitable, good-hearted nephew, who was Dickens' model for what he wanted upper-class people to be.

"Once upon a time—" wrote Dickens, "of all the good days in the year, on Christmas Eve—old Scrooge sat busy in his counting-house. It was cold, bleak, biting weather." Scrooge kept a careful eye on his clerk, Bob Cratchit, to make sure that he burned no more than one ember of coal in a futile attempt to stay warm, and that he did not pause for a moment from his work.

Scrooge's nephew stopped by to wish Scrooge a merry Christmas and to invite him to dine with him and his wife, but Scrooge replied, "Bah! Humbug!" He insisted that there was nothing to celebrate at Christmas, but his nephew responded that it was "a good time; a kind, forgiving, charitable, pleasant time; the only time I know of, in the long calendar of the year, when men and women seem by one consent to open their

Scrooge meets the larger-than-life Ghost of Christmas Present in this famous illustration from the first edition of A Christmas Carol.

shut-up hearts freely, and to think of people below them as if they really were fellow-passengers to the grave . . . and I say, God bless it!"

Two gentlemen approached Scrooge seeking a contribution to help buy food and fuel for the poor, stating, "Many thousands are in want of common necessaries; hundred of thousands are in want of common comforts, sir."

Scrooge replied angrily, "Are there no prisons?"

The gentlemen agreed there were plenty. "'And the Union workhouses?' demanded Scrooge. 'Are they still in operation?'"

The gentlemen protested that no Christmas cheer was to be found there and that many would rather die than go to them. "'If they would rather die,' said Scrooge, 'they had better do it, and decrease the surplus population.'"

Scrooge, as we all know, was in for a fanciful night, full of ghosts and time travel. He returned to his childhood with the Spirit of Christmas Past, and he saw his dismal future with the Spirit of Christmas Yet to Come. Many moments startled and amazed him, helping him to understand how he came to be greedy and unhappy, why it was so wrong, and how it affected the way he would be remembered after death. In an especially dramatic moment he saw two strange shapes emerge from under the long robe worn by the Spirit of Christmas Present. Scrooge realized that they were a boy and a girl, "yellow, meager, ragged, scowling, wolfish." Appalled, he asked, "'Spirit, are they yours?'"

"'They are Man's,' said the Spirit, looking down upon them. 'This boy is Ignorance. This girl is Want. Beware them both, and all of their degree, but most of all beware this boy, for on his brow I see that written which is Doom, unless the writing be erased.'"

"Have they no refuge or resource?" Scrooge asked with concern.

"'Are there no prisons?' responded the Spirit, turning on him for the last time with his own words. 'Are there no work-houses?'"

By the end of the night, Scrooge understood the consequences of poverty on society and his personal obligation to help the poor. He had reconnected with his caring self and, with his icy heart thawed at last, he pleaded with the goulish Spirit of Christmas Yet to Come to let him atone for his sins. He cried, "I will honor Christmas in my heart, and try to keep it all the year. I will live in the Past, the Present, and the Future. The spirits of all three shall strive within me. I will not shut out the lessons that they teach."

When he awoke Christmas morning in his own bed and realized that he did indeed have another chance, he was as good as his word. In fact, "Scrooge was better than his word. He did it all, and infinitely more." During his night's journey he had come to care about Tiny Tim, the crippled son of his clerk, Bob Cratchit, and had been horrified when the Spirit of Christmas Yet to Come had revealed that the boy died because

Tiny Tim, carried on the shoulders of his loving father, Bob Cratchit, proved to be one of Dickens' most enduring and popular characters.

he did not get proper medical attention. Scrooge determined to change this fate. He generously helped the Cratchit family, and particularly Tiny Tim, who soon regained his health.

Scrooge "became as good a friend, as good a master, and as good a man, as the good old city knew, or any other good old city, town, or borough, in the good old world."

Dickens concluded, "It was always said of him, that he knew how to keep Christmas well, if any man alive possessed the knowledge. May that be truly said of us, and all of us! And so, as Tiny Tim observed, God Bless Us, Every One!"

When Dickens finished his story, he was certain his readers would like it. He'd been having some problems with his publishers, and because he felt so confident about his story, he decided to print the first edition at his own cost— a risky venture for someone who hated debt and already owed money. Not only that, he determined that the book should be lavishly produced, with color illustrations and pages with gilt edging. He selected a cover of red cloth with the title stamped in gold. Each of these choices drove up the cost of production—yet Dickens wanted to keep the price affordable, a decision that would severely limit how much money he could make on each copy. If the book did not sell well, he would be financially ruined.

It was the gamble of his career.

A Christmas Carol went on sale the week before Christmas in 1843. Dickens held his breath, waiting to see what would happen. Would reviewers like it? Would people buy it? Then the first review appeared, proclaiming it "a tale to make the reader laugh and cry—open his hands, and open his heart to charity." Word spread quickly, and Dickens' fans lined up. Within four days, the first edition of six thousand copies sold out. Dickens was ecstatic.

The public loved *A Christmas Carol*. Just as Dickens had hoped, people took seriously its messages that the poor genuinely deserved help and that it was never too late to experience redemption and become a better person. And what more appropriate time for these realizations than at Christmas, a holiday celebrating the spirit of goodwill toward all!

On Sunday mornings, ministers used *A Christmas Carol* to illustrate Christian virtues. After reading it, a factory owner gave his laborers an extra holiday. A reader wrote to Dickens, "You may be sure you have done more good by this little publication, fostered more kindly feelings, and prompted more positive acts of beneficence, than can be traced to all the pulpits and confessionals in Christendom."

An American reviewer wrote, "It is one of those stories, the reading of which makes every one better, more contented with life, more resigned to misfortune, more hopeful, more charitable."

Dickens was flooded with letters from ordinary people who told him about themselves and their lives and how meaningful the book was to them. Many mentioned giving the book an honored place in their

A favorite scene from the first edition of the book was the Christmas Eve ball given by Mr. Fezziwig, Scrooge's long-ago employer. The first edition was printed in color, at the time both unusual and expensive.

homes and reading it aloud to their families.

Dickens' warning to the British to beware of man's offspring, Ignorance and Want, did not fall on deaf ears. The wheels of change moved slowly, but by the turn of the century and the end of Victoria's reign in 1901, the reforms that began in Dickens' lifetime had eased the suffering of the poor. While many powerful people were responsible for this, Dickens rightfully received credit, long after he had died, for goading the upper classes to do the right thing—and making them *want* to do it.

━ ▢ ▢ ⌐

Because of printing costs, Dickens did not make the quick money he had hoped, and for a while his finances remained precarious. But through the years *A Christmas Carol* sold very well. It also revived the celebration of Christmas, which became once again a popular, festive holiday. The book nearly put suppliers of geese out of business, however, for in the story, Scrooge sends Bob Cratchit's family the prize turkey hanging in the window of a local poultry shop instead of a traditional goose. Ever since, the British have favored roast turkey over roast goose for their Christmas feast.

Today *A Christmas Carol* is one of literature's most endearing creations. It inevitably appears on lists of "best" and "favorite" stories. "Bah! Humbug!" is part of our language, and we call a miser "Scrooge." All over the world, the story is performed each holiday season on stage. Audiences also gather to hear it being read aloud or to watch one of the many movie adaptations made of it. Dickens' name has become synonymous with a Victorian Christmas—sometimes referred to as a Dickens Christmas—which usually features Dickens carolers singing

Christmas carols and trees decorated with Tiny Tim ornaments. Dickens Christmas festivals are held many places. The most famous is in Rochester, England, the market town Dickens knew so well. In Galveston, Texas, islanders celebrate the end of hurricane season with a Victorian Christmas featuring all things Dickens. The Great Dickens Christmas Fair is an annual event in San Francisco—and on and on the list goes.

Best of all, the popularity of *A Christmas Carol* continues to remind readers of their responsibility to help the less fortunate. It inspires them to honor the spirit of Christmas "all the year," just as Scrooge pledged to do, and to proclaim with Tiny Tim, "God Bless Us, Every One!"

Chapter 14

A Dedicated Reformer

IN DECEMBER 1853, a decade after Charles Dickens had published *A Christmas Carol* to great acclaim—and with his finances in much better shape—he agreed to give a public reading of the story for a society in Birmingham, England, that promoted the education of workers—a special interest of his.

Dickens disliked industrial cities like Birmingham and Manchester, where mountains of slag removed from the mines desecrated the landscape, and black smoke belched from huge industrial smokestacks, darkening the skies. Even though coal dust was a hazard to everyone's health, it was considered part of the price for the industrial revolution that was making England a rich and powerful nation.

As always, the poor carried more than their share of the burden. They lived in the shadows of the smokestacks and breathed in fumes and dust in the mines, factories, and mills. Because of lung damage, few workers older than forty could still hold a job. Most had started working as children, and just reaching forty was an accomplishment. Children comprised one-quarter of Britain's work force. As soon as they were able, they were put to work, their meager earnings helping their families. They toiled alongside children apprenticed to factory owners by orphanages and workhouses, who paid them a pittance to labor twelve to sixteen hours a day, six days a week. Factory children usually slept in decrepit and crowded company barracks.

Child laborers in Victorian England were victimized by uncaring employers who expected them to work long hours for meager wages. They had no opportunity to go to school.

Often boys and girls were assigned the most dangerous tasks to do. The smallest ones had to wiggle into narrow mining shafts far underground and sit hunched over all day, alone, in cold, damp darkness, opening trapdoors for coal cars. Older children carried loads of coal on their backs or pushed coal cars through tunnels too narrow for adults. Sometimes they died in cave-ins or explosions.

In the mills young children were employed to

crawl under machinery to retrieve bobbins or other items that dropped. If they caught a hand, arm, or leg in the machine— well, there was always another child to take the job. In match factories young children spent long days dipping matches into the chemical phosphorus, which caused their teeth to rot and injured their lungs.

Working far underground, children were often assigned the most dangerous jobs in mines. This boy provides the backbreaking labor needed to remove coal from a tunnel.

On and on went the list of abuses, for children were employed everywhere, both indoors and out, working along-side adults in iron and steel mills, manufacturing and textile plants, the building trades, agriculture, and the mines. No legislation protected them from cruel overseers who could beat them, nor were employers required to assist workers, no matter what their ages, who were injured or grew sick. There were no regulations against exposure to toxic chemicals, or cold, wet weather, and often no provision for heat, adequate light, or sanitation, much less safety. Children worked without fresh air or time to play. Because they had no opportunity for education, they had no way to ever better themselves or climb out of poverty.

At the end of a long workday, those with homes returned to slums so squalid that fewer than half the children reached their fifth birthday—the age at which many were put to work.

Dickens had walked through these industrial slums and toured the factories. He knew how hard the lives of all workers were, and when he agreed to visit Birmingham to read aloud *A Christmas Carol,* he requested that one of the readings be reserved for working people, and that they be charged only a small admittance fee.

Two thousand workers jammed the hall the night of his appearance. When Dickens came out on the stage, the local newspaper reported, the audience "rose up and cheered most enthusiastically, and then became quiet again, and then went at it afresh." Dickens addressed them as "My Good Friends," telling them how much he had looked forward to this evening. They responded with "a perfect hurricane of applause" and,

With no laws to protect them, young children like these laborers in a London bobbin factory could be treated very harshly by overseers.

during his reading of *A Christmas Carol,* interrupted him many times with cheers. As always, Dickens was sensitive to their feelings for him. At the end of his reading he told them, "I am truly and sincerely interested in you . . . my little service to you I have freely rendered from my heart." He said of that triumphant evening, "They lost nothing, misinterpreted nothing, followed everything closely, laughed and cried with the most delightful earnestness."

From the time Dickens started to write, England's poor revered him for giving them a voice and status they'd never had before. He was their hero and spokesman. They recognized themselves in his characters and understood that he was not making fun of them but was at work trying to better their lives.

People could ignore blowhard politicians, but as Dickens had proved time and again, his writing had the emotional impact to inspire readers to work for change. He wrote an article about adults and children injured or killed in factory accidents because of unsafe machinery. He toured Manchester's factories and cotton mills and spoke on behalf of the workers and the appalling conditions in which they labored, and he determined that he would "strike the heaviest blow in my power for these unfortunate creatures."

His "heaviest blow" became his dark novel *Hard Times.* Published in 1854, it was set in fictional Cokestown, where industry dominated everything, greed controlled quality of

Small children often worked alongside adults. At least these children making shoes were inside and could sit down.

life, and workers in the mills were expected to obey the will of wealthy factory owners. One of his main characters was Thomas Gradgrind, who believed that everything in life must be regulated and have a purpose. To him, workers were simply pieces of machinery. In Gradgrind's society, personal feelings had to be suppressed for the greater good, and joy and happiness were sins.

Hard Times helped the public understand the terrible human price paid by the working classes, whose role was to serve the rich. Dickens' novel *Bleak House,* published in 1853, also hit on this theme. Set in London, one of its memorable characters was an orphaned child name Jo, a crossing sweep who tried to earn a few coins each day by clearing away the mud, debris, and animal droppings in the way of people walking through the streets or climbing down from carriages. Jo lived in a sordid slum and breathed polluted air. Dickens wanted his readers to experience through Jo the filthy living conditions of the poor, and they were shocked when the child died because of terrible deprivation.

Long before the environmental movement began, Dickens was convinced that pollution created human misery and affected people of every class. He opened *Bleak House* by describing the pollution hanging over London (comparing it to the fog and decay that polluted the British legal court system—another of his targets in this novel). His readers took his message to heart: the novel inspired the cleaning up of one of London's worst slums.

Sickened by industry's destruction of the landscape, the famed British artist J. M. W. Turner painted this scene in 1832 of his hometown, which was surrounded by natural beauty but drowning in pollution.

Dickens also created a vivid picture of London's polluted air in his novel *Great Expectations*. He described the London fog as "smoke lowering down from chimney-pots, making a soft black drizzle, with flakes of soot in it as big as full-grown snowflakes."

In *The Old Curiosity Shop,* published in 1841, he described what visitors saw when approaching one of the industrial cities in the north: "On every side, as far as the eye could see into the heavy distance, tall chimneys . . . poured out their plague of smoke, obscured the light, and made foul the melancholy air."

Over and over in his books he portrayed the problems of pollution and filth. He wrote in the introduction to his novel *Martin Chuzzlewit,* published in 1844, "I hope I have taken every available opportunity of showing the want of sanitary improvements in the neglected dwellings of the poor." As a boy at the blacking factory, Dickens had struggled to stay clean. He knew that being dirty made people feel hopeless and degraded. Influencing legislation to improve the slums was among the most significant work he accomplished in his distinguished career. Rich and poor alike understood the importance of his words when he addressed the Metropolitan Sanitary Commission about this necessity, stating, "Give me my first glimpse of Heaven through a little of its light and air—give me water—help me to be clean."

Dickens did more than write about the poor's need for decent housing. He joined forces with a wealthy philanthropist to clear a foul slum area and build a model housing project for the working poor. The philanthropist financed the project and Dickens oversaw every detail. The end product was four blocks of low-rent dwellings that housed six hundred people. Each family lived in three well-ventilated rooms and had access to washing and bathroom facilities.

Dickens' portrayals of slum life pushed city authorities to undertake improvements, just as his writing had inspired betterment in so many areas of British life. Widespread housing reform would take many more years to become reality, as would cleaning up polluted industrial towns. But change would happen, and the reformers pushing for it often quoted Dickens as their inspiration.

Reform gradually came to regulating child labor as well. When it did, no more five-year-olds were sent down dangerous mineshafts.

Historians sometimes marvel that the lower classes did not openly rebel in England. But during Dickens' lifetime, the upper classes always feared it. Dickens grew up hearing about the French Revolution, which had ended only thirteen years before his birth. He realized that his country was ripe for rebellion by the poor. He did not support this, knowing it would lead to chaos and anarchy, just as it had in France. But how could the upper classes be inspired to create social change that would prevent rebellion?

Dickens warned of it in *A Christmas Carol* with his startling portrayal of the ravenous and sickly girl and boy, representatives of Want and Ignorance, but he wanted to make a much stronger statement.

He did this in *A Tale of Two Cities,* published in 1859, a sprawling novel set against the French Revolution that delivers Dickens' admonition, but is also a great love story, full of violence, intrigue, despair, redemption, and valiant acts of courage. Like all of Dickens' novels, it had a complex plot and a cast of unforgettable characters.

The two cities in the title are London and Paris in the years 1757 to 1793—the period of time leading up to and during the French Revolution. In the novel Dickens portrays both the French and British governments as indifferent to the plight of the poor and guilty of brutality and unjust cruelty toward them.

He began his novel describing England and France with the words "It was the best of times, it was the worst of times, it was the age of wisdom, it was the age of foolishness . . . it was the season of Light, it was the season of Darkness, it was the spring of hope, it was the winter of despair, we had everything before us, we had nothing before us . . . in short, the period was so far like the present period." With his comment "so far like the present period," Dickens gave the British a sharp jab. *Pay attention,* he said. *This could be us!*

With this immensely popular novel, Dickens once again added his influential voice to those of Victorian reformers working for social justice. Though it would happen in other parts of the British Empire, the English would not experience mob rule on their own soil. They were spared the bloody revolutions that tested the very existence of many countries, including France, Russia, and America.

Chapter 15

A Friend to the Poor, a Complex Father

CHARLES DICKENS NEVER LOST his humility. He told an American reporter, "I am trying to enjoy my fame while it lasts, for I . . . am not so foolish as to suppose that my books will be read by any but the men of my own times." His son Henry observed of his father, "To walk with him in the streets of London was a revelation . . . [with] people of all degrees and classes taking off their hats and greeting him as he passed." Even small children, recognizing him from photographs, would cry out, "It's Charles Dickens!" According to Henry, "My father, who had heard and seen it all, was strangely embarrassed; but oh, so pleased, so truly delighted."

Dickens would shake hands with anyone from the high born to the low. He always stopped to talk to small children. He commented, "Wherever I go, I find myself affectionately

cherished in the homes of honest men and women, and associated, as their friend, with their domestic joys and troubles."
He responded personally to what he called "begging letters,"
which he received by the basketful. Even if he declined to
send money, he knew that the receiver could sell his note
with Dickens' signature to a collector and get money that
way. He helped numerous individuals and organizations with
anonymous donations. He arranged medical assistance for sick
children in the slums and helped a number of children attend
Ragged Schools.

Dickens recognized that every day was a struggle for poor people such as this English family photographed in 1857. Throughout his career he portrayed the poor with compassion.

Everyone knew
stories of his kindnesses.
One concerned five
distraught women he
came upon outside a
workhouse one bitter
cold night. The women
could not get into the
workhouse because it
was too full, and they
had nowhere else to go.
Dickens talked to the
master of the workhouse

on their behalf, who assured Dickens that there was no room.
Refusing to leave the women without shelter, Dickens gave
them money for a night's lodging.

He raged against indifferent city officials when a cholera epidemic killed huge numbers of slum children. He wrote a four-part series exposing "baby farmers," who often neglected and starved the children in their care. He wrote vividly of children guilty only of stealing a bit of food to stay alive who were then thrown into prison with violent adults. Over and over he gave his voice to those who could not speak for themselves, forcing people to *see* the invisible poor.

Close to his heart was London's first children's medical hospital, Great Ormond Street Hospital for Sick Children, which opened its doors in 1852 near several of the city's worst slums. It relied entirely on charity for support. Doctors and nurses donated their services. Dickens wrote an article urging people to give generously, and many did. But after six years in operation, the hospital could barely meet half its expenses. Cholera, typhoid fever, measles, malnutrition, and a host of other illnesses killed 20,000 of the city's poorest children every year—yet the hospital had only thirty-one beds.

Dickens was a popular public speaker who always drew crowds. He agreed to give the keynote address at a hospital fundraising dinner, which assured that London's charitable wealthy—the Great and the Good—would come. In his impassioned speech, he hammered home the hospital's role in preventing epidemics and saving lives. To make his listeners *feel* the agonies of sick children, he told the story of a small slum boy, describing him as "a feeble, wasted, wan, sick child . . . with bright attentive eyes. I can see him now, as I have seen him for several years, looking steadily at us. . . . He seldom cried, the mother said; he seldom complained."

According to Dickens, the boy's mother had made him a small bed out of an egg crate she had begged from a merchant. She said her boy seemed to be wondering what it was all about as he lay there, wasting away and slowly dying. "God knows . . . ," said Dickens, "he had his reasons for wondering . . . and why, in the name of a gracious God, should such things be!"

Dickens' audience wept and cheered and then dug deeply into their pockets. This event and a later one, where Dickens read *A Christmas Carol,* raised enough money to secure the hospital's future.

Dickens wrote some of literature's most vivid scenes of happy marriages and family life, but these were only partially reflective of his own. He and Catherine had ten children. A daughter died of illness as a toddler and a son died of illness as a young adult. The other eight—six sons and two daughters—had various difficulties as adults, and most had financial problems. None inherited Dickens' drive or literary gift. The youngest, Edward, observed, "Sons of great men are not usually as great as their fathers. You cannot get two Charles Dickens in one generation."

The children often felt they competed for their father's attention with his fictional characters. When he was in the middle of writing a novel, it could seem to his family as if

Little Nell and Pip and David Copperfield and all the others were his *true* offspring. His eldest son, Charley, commented, "I have often . . . heard him complain that he could not get the people of his imagination to do what he wanted, and that they would insist on working out their history in *their* way and not his. I can very well remember his describing them flocking round the table in the quiet hours . . . each one of them claiming and demanding instant personal attention."

Dickens created more than two thousand characters, many of them beloved by readers. On days when the next installment of one of his novels appeared in a news magazine, fans lined up to buy it. When *The Old Curiosity Shop* was being published, the public started worrying that its sweet young heroine, Little Nell, was going to die. It's said that readers waited on the docks in New York City for the boat bringing copies of the magazine with the next installment of the novel and, as the boat docked, shouted anxiously at passengers, "Is Little Nell dead?"

Dickens did his writing in his study at home. He expected his large household to be very quiet during his work hours. As was typical in upper-middle-class Victorian households, Dickens wanted his to run on a strict schedule, with meals served at a precise time. Servants cared for the children and tutors educated them. They were always well dressed and had excellent manners. They were expected to keep themselves and their surroundings neat and clean.

But Dickens also told them silly stories that made them laugh. He celebrated their birthdays, sang to them and played with them, and was always very gentle and affectionate. He loved to dance, perform magic tricks, and write and act in plays. Every holiday found Dickens hosting family gatherings that included his parents. Until the day John Dickens died, he continued to run up debts that his son had to cover, but both parents were always present at family get-togethers at Dickens' home, where they participated in the dancing, singing, and game playing and were obviously welcome. So were Dickens' siblings and their families. Missing was Dickens' beloved sister Fanny, who had died at age thirty-seven of tuberculosis.

This 1849 sketch shows Catherine Dickens in her early thirties. In spite of her later separation from her husband, she loved him the rest of her life.

Dickens could be loving and funny with his children, but he could also be restless and moody. He gradually grew less affectionate toward his wife. In 1858, after twenty years of marriage, Dickens felt that he and Catherine had grown apart and must separate. There would be no divorce, which would bring public disgrace—a risk Dickens couldn't take with his career. But the marriage was over.

The children, then between the ages of six and nineteen, suffered from

the rupture between their parents and were divided in their loyalties. In 1856 Dickens had been able to buy Gads Hill Place, the home of his childhood dreams, and that became his principal residence. Most of the children and Catherine's sister, who looked after them, remained with Dickens. Catherine, heartbroken by these events, moved to another house but stayed loyal to her husband until his death. The last twelve years of his life, Dickens' companion was a young actress, Ellen Ternan, who was just eighteen when she met the forty-six-year-old author. Little is known about their relationship, for neither of them ever spoke of it publicly.

But Dickens was always secretive about his own life. Only a few friends knew of the difficulties he had suffered as a child. A few months before his death, he was playing a popular memory game with several of his children and he gave the clue "Warren's Blacking, 30 Strand." It meant nothing to the children, for they did not know that at age twelve their father had labored at a factory at that address. Henry Dickens later recalled that his father had offered the clue "with an odd twinkle in his eye and a strange inflection in his voice."

The children would learn the significance of the blacking factory when the rest of the world did—several years after Dickens' death when his close friend John Forster published a biography about him. Forster was one of the few people with whom Dickens had shared his childhood trauma.

Forster had urged Dickens to write his life story, and Dickens tried, getting at least some of it on paper. Perhaps because this brought back such difficult memories, he wrote very little. In Forster's book, he included what Dickens had written about himself. Dickens' most autobiographical novel was *David Copperfield*. Dickens had referred to the title character as "a very complicated interweaving of truth and fiction." Fortunately, Forster knew which passages in this book and also in *Great Expectations* were true, and he identified them.

In both *David Copperfield* and *Great Expectations*, the central characters are boys experiencing difficult childhoods, then growing up and trying to make their way in the world. Like Dickens, David Copperfield began life in the middle class but fell into the working class and had to go to work in a decayed London warehouse on the Thames River. In *Great Expectations*, Pip was part of the working class and was determined to better himself and become a gentleman.

With Forster's guidance, Dickens' family and his public had, at last, important insight into the extremely complex author and why he was passionately devoted to the welfare of poor children.

When Dickens sat for this drawing at age thirty-seven, he was already famous throughout Europe and America. He was very sensitive about his public image and worried that if he divorced his wife, he would lose his fans.

Chapter 16

An Author for the Ages

ON SEVERAL OCCASIONS, Queen Victoria invited Charles Dickens to her palace. He was also asked by the politically powerful to run for Parliament. But Dickens did not want to align himself with a monarch and government that were mostly indifferent to the suffering of the lower classes. Neither would he socialize with the aristocracy who clamored after him, knowing their interest was because of his fame. Instead, he forged close friendships with actors, writers, and artists, and made his home a gathering place for them.

Throughout his career he held up a mirror to Victorian society, forcing the wealthy to see in the reflection its cruelty and indifference toward the poor. He worked magic with his words, becoming one of the greatest reformers of his age. When Oliver Twist says, "Please, sir, I want some more," readers' stomachs growled. Because he made readers care about skinny workhouse orphans and suffering slum children, they gradually opened their hearts to the lower classes and extended a hand up.

Dickens' prolific output included novels, countless stories, essays, editorials, and plays, poetry, and even an opera. In spite of the wealth he accumulated from his writing, his financial worries never left him, for he was generous by nature, and so many people relied on him.

He was constantly asked to read from his works to raise money for various causes, but in the last few years of his life he went on reading tours to make money for himself. He prepared carefully and took on the voices of every character. His presentations were so dramatic—and so thrilling—that on several occasions, audience members fainted. He was in great demand and he drove himself hard, traveling all over England and to other countries, including America. His worried doctors told him he must slow down, that what he was doing was simply too exhausting and was endangering his health. But he enjoyed the readings, and his sold-out audiences loved them and always clamored for more.

In the end, Dickens took it too far. On June 9, 1870, he suffered a fatal stroke at his Gads Hill home. He was fifty-eight years old.

The British were plunged into mourning, and the world grieved with them. In America, Dickens' friend Henry Wadsworth Longfellow commented, "I never knew an author's death to cause such general mourning. It is no exaggeration to say that this whole country is stricken with grief." Tributes poured in. Karl Marx, the philosopher and revolutionary, wrote that

Dickens enjoyed reading aloud from his own works to enthusiastic overflow audiences, but he used up so much energy that he sometimes collapsed afterward. In the last few years of his life, he aged rapidly from overwork and poor health.

Dickens "issued to the world more political and social truths than have been uttered by all the professional politicians, publicists and moralists put together."

Dickens had requested a simple burial with no fuss. But the family bowed to the desire of the government to honor its most beloved writer, and he was buried next to German composer George Frideric Handel in Poets Corner in London's Westminster Abbey. For two long days mourners of every class filed past to view his coffin. Many threw flowers on it. Some were elaborate bouquets and others were bits of twigs and vine tied with rags. Dickens' biographer Peter Ackroyd wrote, "Even to the laboring men and women there was in his death a grievous sense of loss; they felt that he had in large measure understood them and that, in his death, they had also lost something of themselves."

Within a decade of his death, England would have social welfare legislation offering more protection for child laborers. It would also have less pollution, benefiting everybody. Compulsory education would assure that five- to thirteen-year-olds went to school, and all schools became subject to supervision and oversight. Gradually the worst slums disappeared, replaced by affordable housing for the poor. All children had access to education. London became a gleaming world capital, boasting paved streets, modern sewers, wide river embankments, and underground railways. Great Ormond Street Hospital for Sick

Change took time, but London's worst slums gradually gave way to better housing. Overcrowding remained an issue.

Children was able to care for hundreds of patients at a time and it still thrives today. The Foundling Hospital evolved into a strong organization to help families and children in need, telling its story in its own museum, where it honors its founder, Thomas Coram, its great benefactors, George Frideric Handel and the artist William Hogarth, and its good friend Charles Dickens.

Among history's greatest literary figures, Dickens' name is listed alongside Shakespeare's. He was the most widely read author of his time. Soldiers in the American Civil War carried his books to read aloud around nightly campfires. He was more popular in Russia than many of the great Russian novelists. His twenty novels are all still in print, and he remains popular today.

The Victorian Age was named for the queen, but it was Dickens who captured it in print. He is remembered as a teller of stories filled with high drama, evil villains, handsome heroes and beautiful heroines, tug-on-the-heartstrings emotion, laugh-out-loud humor, and some of the most memorable characters in literature, many of whom are children. Unlike any other writer, he gave the lower classes a voice and made them *human* and likable. In his gifted hands, their struggles became readers' struggles. Said one scholar, Dickens presented "the hard facts of hard times in all their light and darkness and [offered to] readers not just a solace for idle hours but a challenge to their sense of right and wrong."

Legions of readers still feel that power. Dickens' books are found in libraries, bookstores, and homes throughout the world, where they continue to entertain and to inspire.

Charles Dickens was truly an author for all the ages.

In the last months of his life Dickens began experiencing problems with his vision. He tired quickly and friends urged him to slow down. His final book, The Mystery of Edwin Drood, *was left unfinished.*

Queen Victoria 1819–1901

Charles Dickens was writing *Oliver Twist* when Victoria was crowned queen of England in 1837, succeeding her uncle, William IV. Born in 1819, she was then eighteen years old. Dickens attended public festivities for her coronation and wrote an article about it.

Many suitors courted the new queen, but she was in love with her first cousin, Prince Albert of Saxe-Coburg. They married in 1840 when they were both twenty-one. The British wanted one of their own as Victoria's husband and were not happy with this German alliance. Prince Albert was shy and studious. He was interested in music, science, and industry. He was active in public life and gradually convinced the British that he was not seeking power or influence, winning them over and gaining their affection.

Victoria was just four foot nine but always insisted she was four eleven. She was plump all her life and had a plain face with a receding chin. She was bossy and stubborn and used to having her own way. After each of her nine children was born, she spiraled into depression. Still, she and Albert were happy together and devoted to each other. She was not fond of babies or young children and did not participate in their care, but Albert doted on them, and the royal family was adored by the public.

The Victorian Age was a time of prosperity for the ever-expanding

This idealized painting shows Victoria and Albert in 1846 with their first five children. Because of Victoria's strong influence on her times, her reign became known as the Victorian Age.

British Empire. As the queen, Victoria did not have a direct role in policy decisions, but she made her views known to her prime ministers, and her influence was important. To help prevent a revolution by the underclasses, it was critical that they be satisfied with her and she proved to be a popular queen. Her subjects admired her straightforward style, her high ethical standards, her modesty, and her optimism. Her courage was evident during seven attempted assassinations on her life.

Even though she eagerly read each new Dickens book, she did little to assist the poor. One exception was sending money to help feed starving Irish during the 1845 potato famine. Otherwise, her position was that the poor should help themselves and that enough charity already existed to care for those who could not. It's said that she was more interested in the welfare of animals than destitute children.

Albert suffered all his life from a bad stomach. He died, probably from stomach cancer, in 1861 when he was forty-two years old. Victoria went into deep mourning for him and wore black in his honor the remaining forty years of her life. Though she continued to carry out her official duties, she stayed in seclusion most of the time until

her own death in 1901 at the age of eighty-two.

Victoria is sometimes referred to as the Grandmother of Europe, for eight of her children married into the royal houses of Europe, including those of Prussia, Denmark, and Russia. These political unions helped to stabilize and unify England and its European allies, though it did not always prevent war. Ironically, one of Victoria's favorite grandsons became Kaiser Wilhelm II of Germany, who would declare war on England at the beginning of World War I.

Victoria was queen for sixty-four years and was England's longest-reigning monarch until 2007, when that record was broken by her great-great-granddaughter, Queen Elizabeth II.

The Legacy of the Workhouse

It wasn't just in *Oliver Twist* that Charles Dickens attacked the workhouses. In a later novel, *Our Mutual Friend*, an elderly character named Betty Higden lost everything she owned. So fearful was she of the workhouse that she set out to try to sell her needlework, traveling from place to place on foot, even in the worst of weather. When she died from this hardship, it was discovered that she had sewn money into her clothing to be used for a proper burial so she wouldn't end up in an unmarked pauper's grave.

Even with Dickens' influence, the workhouses were never satisfactory.

Male residents of a county poor farm in America wait in line for their noon meal in this 1940s photograph.

The last ones did not close until 1930. By then England had created public assistance to aid the poor, including programs to help struggling families stay together. Orphanages cared for homeless children, and adoption became more commonplace.

In the United States before 1800, needy people relied on charity for help. When their numbers became overwhelming, local governments took on their care. Officials realized it would be cheapest and most efficient to put charity cases together in one place, just as it was done in England. The American versions of the workhouse were the poorhouse and poor farm. They could be anything from cramped houses to large institutions. At poor farms, anyone capable of working helped raise food to feed all the inmates. Throughout the rest of the 1800s and as late as the end of World War II in 1945, young and old, poor and sick, lived together in these dismal, depressing places.

The existence of poorhouses and poor farms in America is sometimes referred to as a "hidden" history—one that people want to forget. As in England, abuses of all types were rampant. Counties in some states actually

These boys in India are at work helping to clear a construction site. It's common in India for children as young as six to work as rag pickers, searching through mountains of trash for any items they can sell.

auctioned off the poor to the lowest bidder to work for specified lengths of time. The bidder was supposed to supply shelter, clothing, and medical care in exchange for labor. As with everything pertaining to the welfare of the poor, conditions varied greatly.

Today a variety of government programs assist the poor and disabled with medical care, food, and other benefits. Many are able to live in government-

For a long time, the Foundling Hospital in Paris had a wheel with a basket where a mother could secretly put her infant, then turn the wheel, placing the baby safely inside the Foundling walls.

subsidized housing. Towns and cities have shelters for the homeless and protective services for people in abusive situations. The government oversees the welfare of orphans and children whose families cannot care for them. Most live in small group homes and foster homes. If adoption becomes an option for them, they join their new families with the government's blessing.

Child Labor Today

The United States, England, and most other Western countries have strict laws regarding child labor. But the United Nations estimates that worldwide one in six children under the age of fifteen—a total of 150 million children in all—works full time.

Charles Dickens wrote about nineteenth-century Victorian England, but many children around the world still live and work in conditions as bad as anything he described. They labor in hazardous conditions and are the targets of abuse and exploitation. Few of these children are able to go to school, and most will live their lives in poverty. International organizations are trying to help protect and educate child laborers but often run into indifference or resistance from governments, local authorities, and parents.

Foundlings and Street Children Worldwide

By the time Thomas Coram started the London Foundling Hospital in 1741, similar institutions already existed all over Europe, usually operated by religious groups. Most foundling hospitals had a designated safe place where infants could be left by parents who then disappeared. Some of the hospitals were terrible. In Ireland, then a very poor country, the workhouse and foundling hospital in Dublin were combined into one huge institution where conditions were so awful that almost every child died. Others, such as the foundling hospital in Paris, were exemplary.

Italy was unusual in that every major city had a foundling hospital. In Venice, the foundling hospital known as the Pieta was supported by wealthy patrons. The Pieta children's choir and orchestra were renowned all over Europe. The famous composer Vivaldi, a priest, was the Pieta's music director for forty years and wrote compositions that the children performed.

In the United States, the New York City Foundling Hospital opened in 1867 to care for orphaned and abandoned babies. It joined the Children's Aid Society in sponsoring orphan trains beginning in the 1850s. Throughout the United States, abandoned and orphaned children grew up in orphanages run by the government or religious groups.

Today, a small group of countries, among them Russia, Romania, Korea, China, Vietnam, and several Latin American nations, allow their orphans to be adopted by families in other countries. For Chinese children, this has saved lives. Once, every town in China had a "dying hill" where unwanted infants were left to die. Many other Chinese children were abandoned as a result of war, poverty, and the government's single-child-per-family policy imposed as a way to control population growth. The current preference for boys over girls means that Chinese orphanages struggle to care for huge numbers of abandoned girls and also abandoned disabled boys. But because Chinese law now permits overseas adoption, many of these children have been able to find families in other countries.

The United States is one of the countries that permit its citizens to adopt internationally. Nearly 300,000 foreign children have been adopted by Americans since the 1950s. Ironically,

Students at an art school in London donated their time and talent to aid African street children.

nearly 1.5 million American children are in foster care, many of them desperate for adoptive homes. As has always been the case, healthy newborns are the most likely to be chosen by adoptive families—whether from this country or another. Older children and sibling groups are usually the last to be chosen. Many countries have programs to assist poor families so they are able to keep their children with them.

Reliable birth control, greater acceptance of single-parent families, and more government assistance to poor parents have decreased child abandonment in many countries. But in others it's still a major problem. No one knows actual numbers, but there may be as many as 100 million street children worldwide. In India alone, there are at least 11 million, and the actual figure may be considerably higher.

In Africa, an estimated 35 million orphans have lost their parents to AIDS, and many of these children live on the streets. In any South or Central American city, hordes of homeless children search daily for food and shelter. In other places the numbers are much smaller, but children are still homeless and trying to care for themselves.

In Charles Dickens' time, children were considered property. Today, the United Nations promotes human rights for children through UNICEF. To ensure the safety and survival of children whose parents might harm them, some countries allow a woman to check in to a hospital anonymously to give birth, then leave without her child. In the United States, parents can leave their children in designated "safe havens," such as hospitals and police stations, without fear of prosecution.

Such safety nets save innocent lives.

What Charles Dickens wrote 170 years ago remains true today: life is difficult for the poor—and is most difficult of all for poor children.

How You Can Make a Difference

Few of us can do as much to help those in need as Bono, the Irish musician known for his charitable concerts that help fight poverty and hunger worldwide. But thanks to the Internet, it's not difficult to assist the world's impoverished children—every contribution, no matter how small, will help—as long as you connect with reliable organizations. Here are some possibilities.

The organization www.FightFor-TheChildren.org provides medical care and educational scholarships for children in developing countries.

Organizations such as the Invisible Children (www.invisiblechildren.com) are raising awareness about child soldiers in places like Uganda and are raising money to build schools in poor countries. Small sums of money collected by students help poor people purchase farm animals through several organizations, including Heifer International (www.heifer.org).

Groups and individuals sponsor underprivileged children in needy countries (www.SavetheChildren.org; www.WorldVision.org) and contribute to organizations that help provide necessary medical care (www.doctorswithoutborders.com). Some individuals help support organizations with specific causes, like www.smiletrain.org, which provides surgery for children born with a cleft palate.

The United Nations Refugee Agency attempts to help children all over the world who are displaced by war and famine. To learn more, go to www.unhcr.org. And you'll find out about street children worldwide and how to help them at streetkidnews.blogsome.com.

In addition to raising money, you can contribute your time and talents to helping the less fortunate. Locally, community organizations that sponsor food pantries and serve meals to the poor always need help, as do shelters for the homeless and victims of domestic violence. Or use your artistic talents to call attention to programs and people desperate for assistance. Individuals and groups sometimes pool resources to sponsor AIDS orphans in Africa, or they collect new and used clothing for children on American Indian reservations.

Charles Dickens and other reformers you've read about in this book can be your inspiration. They proved the power of one, and so can you. There's a world of need out there, and *you* can make a difference.

More About Charles Dickens and His Times

Life in Charles Dickens's England by Diane Yancey (San Diego: Lucent Books, 1999) provides a historical context for the Industrial Revolution, poverty, and child labor.

Charles Dickens: The Man Who Had Great Expectations by Diane Stanley and Peter Vennema (New York: Morrow Junior Books, 1993) offers an illustrated look at the life of Dickens. Young readers will enjoy adapted and illustrated editions of Dickens' novels, while older and more advanced readers will be ready for the originals. Particularly recommended are *Oliver Twist, A Christmas Carol, Great Expectations,* and *David Copperfield.* Peter Ackroyd's biography, titled *Dickens* (New York: Harper Perennial, 1992), is for serious students and adults who want a definitive account of Dickens' life.

Recommended Websites

charlesdickenspage.com. An all-purpose website, full of helpful information about Dickens and his works. The section "Dickens on the Web" includes links to all the major websites about Dickens.

victorianweb.org. Comprehensive information about the Victorian Age. Click on "Authors" and then "Charles Dickens" for more about the author.

lang.nagoya-u.ac.jp/~matsuoka/ Dickens.html. A scholarly site with an excellent search feature of anything related to Dickens.

www.spartacus.schoolnet.co.uk. A British website about history that offers excellent resources for students. For more on workhouse children, including stories in their own words, click on the link "Child Labor 1750–1900" and go to "Workhouse Children."

www.foundlingmuseum.org.uk. Historical information about the Foundling Hospital in London and photos of the children.

Notes

3. THE EARLY YEARS

20 "he watched night and day": Dickens, *My Early Times*, p. 77.

"I thought it was the most": Dickens, *My Early Times*, p. 52.

22 "within a single year": Dickens, *My Early Times*, p. 78.

"appeared to have utterly lost": Dickens, *My Early Times*, p. 77.

23 "making myself useful in the work": Dickens, *My Early Times*, p. 78.

"We got on very badly": Dickens, *My Early Times*, p. 78.

24 "My father and mother were quite satisfied": Dickens, *My Early Times*, p. 80.

4. A WORKING-CLASS BOY

25 "No words can express": Dickens, *My Early Times*, p. 77.

26 "crazy, tumble-down old house": Dickens, *My Early Times*, p. 80.

"I really thought his heart": Dickens, *My Early Times*, p. 82.

27 "Almost everything, by degrees": Dickens, *My Early Times*, p. 83.

28 "no advice, no counsel": Dickens, *My Early Times*, p. 86.

30 "I never said": Dickens, *My Early Times*, p. 87.

"Bob Fagin settled him": Dickens, *My Early Times*, p. 88.

31 "Bob Fagin was very good to me": Dickens, *My Early Times*, p. 88.

31 "But Bob . . . did not like the idea": Dickens, *My Early Times*, p. 89.

32 "When I had money enough": Dickens, *My Early Times*, p. 87.

33 "I know I do not exaggerate": Dickens, *My Early Times*, p. 87.

5. GROWING UP

34 "I could not bear to think of myself": Dickens, *My Early Times*, p. 86.

35 "Bob Fagin and I": Dickens, *My Early Times*, p. 94.

"I wondered how he could bear it": Dickens, *My Early Times*, p. 94.

"My father said I should go back": Dickens, *My Early Times*, p. 95.

"It seemed to me so long": Dickens, *My Early Times*, p. 96.

39 "I never had the courage": Dickens, *My Early Times*, p. 95.

40 "a very small and not": Dickens, *My Early Times*, p. xxi.

"I knew I was common": Dickens, *Great Expectations*, p. 70.

"wander desolately back": Dickens, *My Early Times*, p. 81.

6. BECOMING A WRITER

42 "a mob of brainless windbags": Stanley, *Charles Dickens*, p. 11.

43 "It is to the wholesome training": Dickens, *My Early Times*, p. 124.

"I had taken, with fear and trembling": Dickens, *My Early Times*, p. 142.

44 "I walked down to Westminster Hall": Dickens, *My Early Times*, p. 142.

45 "A brutal laugh at her weak voice": Dickens, "The Streets of London at Night," www.cityofshadows.net.

"die of cold and hunger": Dickens, "The Streets of London at Night," www.cityofshadows.net.

7. THE WORKHOUSE

50 "I walked . . . that Sunday morning": Dickens, "A Walk in the Workhouse," www.victorianweb.org/authors/dickens/poorlaw.html.

52 "often found under the charge": Elizabeth Robins, "Votes for Women," www.Spartacus.schoolnet.co.uk/Lpoor1834.htm.

53 "I was horrified to see little girls": Emmeline Pankhurst, *My Own Story*, www.spartacus.schoolnet.co.uk/Lpoor1834.htm.

8. *OLIVER TWIST*

55 "Let me see the child and die": Dickens, *Oliver Twist*, p. 4.

"She was brought here last night": Dickens, *Oliver Twist*, p. 5.

"The old story": Dickens, *Oliver Twist*, p. 5.

56 "the workhouse authorities": Dickens, *Oliver Twist*, p. 6.

"a woman of wisdom and experience": Dickens, *Oliver Twist*, p. 6.

"found him a pale, thin child": Dickens, *Oliver Twist*, p.7.

"You have come here to be educated": Dickens, *Oliver Twist*, p. 13.

57 "What an illustration of the tender laws": Dickens, *Oliver Twist*, p.13.

"A council was held": Dickens, *Oliver Twist*, p. 14.

"the boys whispered to each other": Dickens, *Oliver Twist*, p. 15.

58 "bruised three or four boys": Dickens, *Oliver Twist*, p. 21.

"stagnant and filthy": Dickens, *Oliver Twist*, p. 41.

59 "A dirtier or more wretched place": Dickens, *Oliver Twist*, p. 63.

60 "truly happy": Dickens, *Oliver Twist*, p. 453.

62 "It's all among workhouses": Dickens, *Oliver Twist*, p. xiii.

"excessively interesting": Dickens, *Oliver Twist*, p. xiii.

9. THE SEA CAPTAIN WHO RESCUED FOUNDLING CHILDREN

67 "Hospital for the Maintenance": Jocelyn, *A Home for Foundlings*, p. 17.

68 "a more moving scene": Pugh, *London's Forgotten Children*, p. 34.

70 "Go gentle babe, and all thy life": Coram Family Annual Review 2006, p. 2.

72 "We were always hungry": Jocelyn, *A Home for Foundlings*, p. 51.

"We weren't going to be wonderful": Jocelyn, *A Home for Foundlings*, p. 59.

73 "We were guilty and we *felt* guilty": Adie, *Nobody's Child*, p. 115.

10. THE GREAT BENEFACTORS: HANDEL, HOGARTH, AND DICKENS

82 "miserable reality": Dickens, *My Early Times*, p. 156.

83 "the moralist and censor of his age": Dickens, *My Early Times*, p. 158.

84 "I painted with most pleasure": Pugh, *London's Forgotten Children*, p. 73.

"The [blank] day of the [blank]": Pugh, *London's Forgotten Children*, p. 83.

"trained out of their blank state": Pugh, *London's Forgotten Children*, p. 83.

85 "Does any wretched mother ever come here": Dickens, *Little Dorrit*, p. 18.

11. CLOSING ENGLAND'S WORST SCHOOLS

87 "ripped it open with an inky pen-knife": Ackroyd, *Dickens*, p. 250.

"The impression made on me never left me": Dickens, *My Early Times*, p. 164.

89 "was by far the most ignorant man": Dickens, *My Early Times*, p. 97.

91 "the lowest and most rotten": Dickens, *My Early Times*, p. 164.

"a very sinister appearance": Yancey, *Life in Charles Dickens's England*, p. 54.

92 "Mr. Squeers is the representative": Dickens, *Nicholas Nickleby*, preface, p. lvi.

"wholly failed to discover an example": Ackroyd, *Dickens*, p. 357.

92 "a national abuse": Ackroyd, *Dickens*, p. 257.

"the monstrous neglect of education": Dickens, *Nicholas Nickleby*, p. liii.

12. SENDING RAGGED CHILDREN TO SCHOOL

94 "doomed childhood": Ackroyd, *Dickens*, p. 407.

"a helping hand is held out": Paterson, *Voices from Dickens-London*, p. 211.

96 "I go to a Ragged School": Picard, *Victorian London*, p. 237.

98 "look forward . . . to another life": Yancey, *Life in Charles Dickens's England*, p. 60.

"intense and prolonged": Ackroyd, *Dickens*, p. 405.

"I have very seldom seen": Ackroyd, *Dickens*, p. 405.

"The name implies the purpose": Dickens, letter to the editor of the *Daily News*, www.victorianlondon.org/education/raggedschools.htm.

"appreciation of the efforts of these teachers": Dickens, www.charlesdickenspage.com/field_lane_ragged_school.html.

102 "They know what it is to have no fire": Ridge, *Dr. Barnardo and the Copperfield Road Ragged Schools*, p. 7.

13. GIVING FROM A CHARITABLE HEART

106 "reluctant to lay it aside": Standiford, *The Man Who Invented Christmas*, p. 84.

106 "this ghostly little book": Dickens, preface to *A Christmas Carol,* p. 3.

"Marley was dead, to begin with": Dickens, *A Christmas Carol,* p. 9.

"a squeezing, wrenching, grasping": Dickens, *A Christmas Carol,* p. 10.

107: "Once upon a time": Dickens, *A Christmas Carol,* p.11.

"Bah! Humbug": Dickens, *A Christmas Carol,* p. 12.

"a good time; a kind, forgiving, charitable": Dickens, *A Christmas Carol,* p. 13.

108 "Many thousands are in want": Dickens, *A Christmas Carol,* p. 16.

"yellow, meager, ragged": Dickens, *A Christmas Carol,* p. 84.

109 "I will honor Christmas in my heart": Dickens, *A Christmas Carol,* p. 107.

"Scrooge was better than his word": Dickens, *A Christmas Carol,* p. 117.

110 "became as good a friend": Dickens, *A Christmas Carol,* p. 117.

"It was always said of him": Dickens, *A Christmas Carol,* p. 119.

111 "a tale to make the reader": Standiford, *The Man Who Invented Christmas,* p. 131.

"You may be sure you have done more good": Standiford, *The Man Who Invented Christmas,* p. 160.

112 "It is one of those stories": Standiford, *The Man Who Invented Christmas,* p. 139.

114 "all the year": Dickens, *A Christmas Carol,* p. 107.

"God Bless Us, Every One": Dickens, *A Christmas Carol,* p. 119.

14. A DEDICATED REFORMER

118 "rose up and cheered most enthusiastically": Ackroyd, *Dickens,* p. 684.

119 "I am truly and sincerely interested in you": Ackroyd, *Dickens,* p. 685.

"They lost nothing": Ackroyd, *Dickens,* p. 684.

"strike the heaviest blow": Ackroyd, *Dickens,* p. 273.

121 "smoke lowering down from chimney-pots": Paterson, *Voices from Dickens' London,* p. 19.

"On every side, as far as the eye": Yancey, *Life in Charles Dickens's England,* p. 81.

122 "I hope I have taken every available opportunity": "Dickens' War on Filth," www.guardian.co.uk/media/2005/oct/20/broadcasting.bbc.

"Give me my first glimpse of Heaven": "Dickens' War on Filth," www.guardian.co.uk/media/2005/oct/20/broadcasting.bbc.

124 "It was the best of times": Dickens, *A Tale of Two Cities,* p. 7.

15. A FRIEND TO THE POOR, A COMPLEX FATHER

125 "I am trying to enjoy my fame while it lasts": Ackroyd, *Dickens,* p. 286.

126 "To walk with him in the streets of London": Ackroyd, *Dickens,* p. 853.

"My father, who had heard and seen it all": Ackroyd, *Dickens,* p. 852.

"Wherever I go, I find myself affectionately cherished": Ackroyd, *Dickens,* p. 855.

128 "a feeble, wasted, wan": Ackroyd, *Dickens,* p. 801.

"God knows": Ackroyd, *Dickens,* p. 801.

129 "Sons of great men are not usually as great": Ackroyd, *Dickens,* p. 878.

"I have often . . . heard him complain that he": Ackroyd, *Dickens,* pp. 400–401.

132 "with an odd twinkle in his eye": Ackroyd, *Dickens,* p. 1057.

"a very complicated": Standiford, *The Man Who Invented Christmas,* p. 207.

16. AN AUTHOR FOR THE AGES

134 "Please, sir, I want some more": *Oliver Twist,* p. 15.

135 "I never knew an author's death to cause": Ackroyd, *Dickens,* p. xviii.

136 "issued to the world": Ackroyd, *Dickens,* p. 720.

"Even to the laboring men and women": Ackroyd, *Dickens,* p. xiv.

138 "the hard facts of hard times": Brown, *Dickens in His Time,* p. 16.

Selected Bibliography

Ackroyd, Peter. *Dickens*. New York: Harper Perennial, 1992.

Adie, Kate. *Nobody's Child*. London: Hodder & Stoughton, 2005.

Brown, Ivor. *Dickens in His Time*. London: Thomas Nelson and Sons, 1953.

Coram Family Annual Review 2006. London: Coram Family, 2006.

Dickens, Charles. *Bleak House*. Boston: Houghton Mifflin, 1956.

———. *A Christmas Carol*. New York: Barnes & Noble Books, 2003.

———. *David Copperfield*. New York: Signet Classics, 1962.

———. *Great Expectations*. New York: Holt, Rinehart and Winston, 1963.

———. *Hard Times*. New York: Bantam Dell, 2004.

———. *Little Dorrit*. Oxford: Oxford University Press, 1994.

———. *My Early Times*. Compiled and edited by Peter Rowland. London: Aurum Press, 1988.

———. *Nicholas Nickleby*. New York: Alfred A. Knopf, 1993.

———. *Oliver Twist*. London: Penguin Books, 2002.

———. *A Tale of Two Cities*. London: Signet Classics, 2007.

Jocelyn, Marthe. *A Home for Foundlings*. Toronto: Tundra Books, 2005.

Paterson, Michael. *Voices from Dickens' London*. Cincinnati: David & Charles, 2006.

Picard, Liza. *Victorian London: The Tale of a City 1840–1870*. New York: St. Martin's Press, 2005.

Pugh, Gillian. *London's Forgotten Children: Thomas Coram and the Foundling Hospital*. Glouchestershire, England. Tempus Publishing, 2007.

Ridge, T. S. *Dr. Barnardo and the Copperfield Road Ragged Schools*. London: Ragged School Museum Trust, 2002.

Standiford, Les. *The Man Who Invented Christmas*. New York: Crown Publishers, 2008.

Stanley, Diane, and Peter Vennema. *Charles Dickens: The Man Who Had Great Expectations*. New York: Morrow Junior Books, 1993.

Yancey, Diane. *Life in Charles Dickens's England*. San Diego: Lucent Books, 1999.

Works Consulted

Gaunt, William. *The World of William Hogarth*. London: Jonathan Cape, 1978.

Hogwood, Christopher. *Handel*. London: Thames & Hudson, 2007.

May, Trevor. *The Victorian Workhouse*. Buckinghamshire, England: Shire Publications, 1997.

Mitchell, Sally. *Daily Life in Victorian England*. Westport, Conn.: Greenwood Press, 1996.

Pool, Daniel, *What Jane Austen Ate and Charles Dickens Knew*. New York: Touchstone Books, 1993.

Richardson, John. *London & Its People: A Social History from Medieval Times to the Present Day*. London: Barrie & Jenkins, Random House, 1995.

St. John Parker, Michael. *Life in Victorian Britain*. Norwich, England: Pitkin Guides, Jarrold Publishing, 1999.

———. *The World of Dickens*. Norwich, England: Pitkin Guides, Jarrold Publishing, 1999.

Thomas, Donald. *The Victorian Underworld*. New York: New York University Press, 1998.

Wilson, A. N. *The Victorians*. New York: W.W. Norton, 2003.

www.cityofshadows.net.

www.guardian.co.uk/media.

www.spartacus.schoolnet.co.uk/Lpoor1834.htm.

www.victorianweb.org/authors/dickens/poorlaw.html.

Major Works by Charles Dickens

Sketches by Boz (1836)

Pickwick Papers
(serialized monthly 1836–37)

Oliver Twist
(serialized monthly 1837–39)

Nicholas Nickleby
(serialized monthly 1838–39)

The Old Curiosity Shop
(serialized weekly 1840–41)

Barnaby Rudge
(serialized weekly 1841)

Martin Chuzzlewit
(serialized monthly 1843–44)

Dombey and Son
(serialized monthly 1846–48)

David Copperfield
(serialized monthly 1849–50)

Bleak House
(serialized monthly 1852–53)

Hard Times
(serialized weekly 1854)

Little Dorrit
(serialized monthly 1855–57)

A Tale of Two Cities
(serialized weekly 1859)

Great Expectations
(serialized weekly 1860–61)

Our Mutual Friend
(serialized monthly 1864–65)

The Mystery of Edwin Drood—unfinished
(serialized monthly 1870)

A Note to Readers

In writing this book I have made every attempt to verify information. My sources include what Charles Dickens wrote, along with what has been written about him, the age he lived in, and other institutions and reformers working to help the poor. I also interviewed experts about Dickens, London, the Foundling Hospital, Queen Victoria, the Victorian Age, and British history.

While I was living in London, I took a walking tour one day that was titled "The London Foundling." This was when I learned of Dickens' tremendous impact on the street children of London. I set to work learning everything I could about Dickens while I was there. I became a member of the Foundling Museum so I could have access not only to its displays but to its expert staff. During several visits to the museum I saw the copy of *Messiah* left to the Foundling by Handel and studied the paintings given by Hogarth, including his famous portrait of Thomas Coram.

I also visited the Charles Dickens Museum, which is located very near the Foundling Hospital in the first London home Dickens owned. Working with an archivist on staff, I was able to view letters and notes Dickens had written and also see first editions of his books and original family photos. In the upstairs study where Dickens wrote *Oliver Twist* and *Nicholas Nickleby* I saw his prized Hogarth prints. I also visited other London museums to explore their Dickens' collections.

In addition to my research at the British Library in London, I read dozens of books and articles written by Dickens scholars worldwide. Especially helpful to me were those by Peter Ackroyd, Ivor Brown, and Les Standiford.

If you go to London today, you will find traces of Charles Dickens, just as I did. The city changed dramatically during his lifetime and has changed dramatically since, but you will still come across narrow lanes of ancient brick and cobblestone. The Victorian era slums and the blacking factory are gone, but many places associated with Dickens are still there in the oldest parts of the city—the Inns of Court, Saint Paul's Cathedral, Westminster Abbey where Dickens is buried, Fleet Street and the Strand, various pubs he frequented, London Bridge and London Tower. You can visit Great Ormond Street Hospital with its famed statue of Peter Pan in the courtyard, and you can spend several fascinating hours at the Foundling Museum, where you'll see some of the identifying tokens left by mothers surrendering their children, and you'll hear taped recordings of Foundling children telling of their experiences there.

I also took in the annual Dickens Festival one Saturday in December in Rochester. Dickens lived close to this market town as a child and again as an adult. When I was there, I admired the ancient Norman castle and the lovely old cathedral and looked out at the Medway River just as I knew Dickens had once done. Townspeople dressed as characters from Dickens' novels paraded through the very streets that Dickens once strolled. Vendors hawked such Victorian delicacies as hot toddies and roasted chestnuts. Bagpipe music filled the air, as did artificial snow. The day ended with a candlelight caroling service at Rochester Cathedral.

Back in London I visited the Ragged School Museum on Copperfield Road in East London. Here I got insight into what life was like for the slum children who struggled to come to school to better themselves.

When I walked along the Thames River that flows through the city, I thought about what London had been like during Dickens' lifetime, with filthy streets encased in the smog that perpetually hung in the air. Looking at the water, I could picture ragged boys and girls searching for anything they could sell to earn a few pennies and keep hunger at bay for one more day.

I imagined Charles Dickens watching them, pulling out his notebook and scribbling down words that might appear in his next book—words that would inspire others to help these children to have a better life. From all I learned and have shared with you in this book, he truly was the best friend poor children ever had.

Acknowledgments

With this book, our seventh together, I am once again indebted to my agent, Regina Ryan, who from the very beginning has steadfastly believed in and supported my vision as a writer. I am deeply grateful to Melanie Kroupa, who saw me through the first draft, instilling it with her wisdom. I am thankful to my editor, Erica Zappy, who loves Dickens, and her colleagues at Houghton Mifflin Harcourt for embracing this project and bringing it to life. I will always be grateful to Pat and Jack Ricard, who conspired to get me to London, which in turn made this book possible, and I'm thankful to Patti Hoddinott, who tramped around that fascinating city with me and took a lively interest in my research. Of invaluable help was the great British Library, where the dedicated staff offered this Yank research assistance with source material I would not have found in United States libraries. Finally, to my family: you are the inspiration that keeps me grounded and lets me know that all will be well, even when dark overshadows the light, and for that and all else, I love you.

Index ⌐☐☐⌐ Page numbers in *italics* refer to illustrations.